I0788142

# SATAN'S SISTER

## RUBY JEAN JENSEN

Gayle J. Foster

# STEP SISTER

*Ellen was only two years old the first time her agonized screams brought the family running. They found the baby cornered, clawed welts on her face turning angry purple, blood streaming from a series of vicious jabs on her forearm. All the while Mary Lou, her step-sister torturer, smothered the infant's wails with one hand and lashed out at her, using blunt cut-out scissors.*

*And now, over two decades later, the outcast hellcat had returned to finish what she started.*

# CHAPTER 1

In the half-light of the midnight dark and stillness of the large, old room the waking girl saw her. She was standing at the foot of the bed, her teeth gleaming in the moonlight that streaked across her small face. She was laughing so silently, ever so silently as she watched the wakening terror. Her black hair fell down the sides of her cheeks, scraggly, uncombed, making her face a white diamond in the night. The scream of the girl in the bed broke through at last, and the visitor faded into the darkness.

It was the nightmare again.

Ellen's eyes searched the room frantically, reaching into the dark shadows of the corners, into shadows behind large old pieces of furniture that had been in the room since the house was built over a hundred years ago. Furniture that could conceal the small, thin body of a nine- or ten-year-old child. The nightmare girl was still there; she could feel her eyes, hear the echo of her taunting laughter. She was hiding. Ready to jump out with her hands shaped into claws over her head, her white teeth bared, her lips drawn back, making her diamond face a mask grotesque and terrible.

The thought of these things had sent Ellen Crayley screaming to her grandmother when she was six, and even when she was sixteen. But now, having passed her twentieth birthday she had to face the truth. Even at midnight when the moonlight was thin and cold and the prairie wind blew sand against the windows. Even with the spirit of the tormenting girl still there, somewhere. It was only a nightmare that recurred when she least expected it, sometimes months apart, sometimes even a year or more. Though actually afraid to reach out her arm, she leaned over and snapped on the bedside lamp, and the shadows were revealed. Hiding no one, of course.

She still trembled, and the large, old-fashioned bedroom held the spirit of the small tormentor even with the lights on. Ellen slipped her feet into sturdy house shoes and got the heavy robe off the foot of the bed. The room was cold. There was no central heating in the old house, and little heat at all in the third story. When she was a child she had loved the height of her bedroom. To look out the windows was to feel as if she lived above all the world. Above even the mountains in the west. But tonight, and those other nights when she had run from the nightmare girl, the stairway down was narrow, long, too steep, and treacherously dark.

She paused on the second floor and looked toward the door of her grandmother's room, but Granny had grown old and feeble and rested poorly. To wake her would be childish and unkind. She went on through the long, dark hall of the second floor, one hand touching the wall for guidance, past other closed doors and rooms no longer occupied. The old Crayley house had held several generations, but the family had gradually grown smaller. Tonight there was no one in the house but Granny, herself, and Miss Maud.

Ellen opened the door to the back stairs and saw that Miss Maud, the housekeeper, had left a night light in the hall by the kitchen. Warmth was there, coming from the big iron cookstove. She slowed, moved quietly through the hall, kitchen, and across the wide screened porch at the back of the house. Miss Maud was several years younger than Granny, but woke easily too. She was thin and nervous, and had come to live in and keep the Crayley house when Ellen was still a small child. Her rooms were just off the far end of the kitchen, and Ellen didn't want to wake her.

The wind nearly tore the door from Ellen's hands, but she held on to it and fought to close it quietly, and won. Then she turned, her eyes going toward the low hill just north of the barns where the moon spread pale light over tops of cedars and turned to whiten the gray, scattered tombstones of the family graveyard. Ellen didn't mind the wind. It had blown sand from around the cedars almost ceaselessly as long as she could remember, and blown it back again so that a root was seldom exposed, a tombstone never covered or uncovered. The wind blew her hair back from her face tonight because it swept fierce down the hillside. She lifted her face toward it and took a deep breath. Then she was running, her robe whipping in the wind, her hair swept back and shining in the moonlight. She crossed the alfalfa meadow where for a while the wind was held aside by the hill, then she climbed, going among the cedars, passing the grave of her grandfather.

On the top of the hill she stopped. North lay cattle range, and the wind rolled a tumbleweed up to her, past her, where it lodged in a cedar. She stood in the center of the graveyard. Her young uncle, Lance, used to try to scare her from going there. But she had never been afraid of the graveyard. She had never been afraid of anything but the nightmare. Her mother's grave was to the right and slightly downhill at the edge of the cedars. Although it was seventeen years old, it was the family's most recent grave.

She went to it and sat down beside the tall gray stone. Next to Granny, and sometimes even more than Granny, it had been her source of comfort. She loved and admired her father, but as the eldest Crayley, president of the bank of Crayley, on the board of nearly everything in Crayley County, he was too busy to be bothered. The reason she and Granny were alone now was because of business in South America. Something about a new breed of cattle. She wasn't even sure. He had called her home from college to stay with her grandmother while he was gone. He was from the old school of men who thought that a college education was not necessary for a woman. He had never really approved of her leaving home in the first place. She had been glad to come home, but she couldn't help thinking about the oddity of the nightmare coming again after three years of freedom from it.

The cold stone against her back calmed her and she stopped trembling, but her gaze moved back and found the tall, ugly house that was known all over the county as the Crayley mansion. Moonlight glinted against the windows of her room high up under the peaked roof, and on the lower roof that slanted steeply down beneath it. There were only three rooms on the top floor and, in all her memory, the other two had not been occupied. The rest of the family slept on the second floor where eleven bedrooms more than filled the need. For the first time she wondered why she alone occupied the third floor. She must ask, she thought. And maybe even ask permission to move downstairs.

She turned her face north again and pressed one cheek against the stone. A few years ago she would have carried on a one-sided conversation with her mother, telling her hopes, her longings, her fears, asking advice; but in recent years, during her vacations at home, she came to the hill merely because it seemed the most peaceful place she knew. A place where she could relax and be at rest. The feeling that her relatives were all about her had been put aside with her childhood. She sat alone now with the gray tombstones, the dark cedars, and the tumbleweeds that bounded lightly up the hill toward her. For several minutes she sat, growing colder, knowing she should go back to the house. But she didn't want to go upstairs. Of course she could get a blanket from the linen closet and stay downstairs on a sofa.

A pale light came on in the bunkhouse, a long building west of the barns. It housed the ranch manager and the men who worked the ranch. The light meant it was four o'clock and Mr. Miller, who had been there so long he seemed a natural part of the ranch, was up and about, cooking breakfast for the men.

Ellen got to her feet, feeling half frozen, and went back toward the house.

She was walking as quietly as she could down the second floor hall to the closet near the end when a voice called to her.

"Ellen?"

She stopped. "Yes, Granny?"

"What on earth are you doing up at this hour? You came up from downstairs, didn't you? Come in here. Turn on the light."

"All right."

Ellen opened the heavy door of her grandmother's corner room and switched on the light. The old lady's wrinkled face peeped from the great, high bed like one small raisin on a tray. Ellen went to the bed and gave herself a boost up and sat with her legs swinging. "Aren't you sleeping well, Granny?"

"Oh yes, off and on. But what are you doing up?"

"I was just going for a blanket."

The old lady's eyes, folded into the wrinkles, were dim but searching, revealing a mind untainted by age. "That old nightmare again?"

"Yes."

"Well, why didn't you tell me?"

"I didn't want to disturb you."

"Pshaw. What am I here for? I was hoping maybe you'd grown out of those. You haven't had one for two or three years now, have you?"

"No. None at all while I was away at school. It makes me wonder if there is something about my bedroom that causes me to dream that particular dream." Ellen looked at her hands, smoothed the cuticle back from naturally pink, long nails. "Granny, may I ask a question?"

"Of course."

"Why has my bedroom always been up there?"

"Oh, family custom, I guess." She paused a moment, and then said, "No, that's wrong. The third floor was always reserved for guests until your dad married. Your mother wanted her room up there, so naturally you were put in an adjoining room."

Ellen looked up, surprised. "But Dad's room is down here!"

"Only since your mother died. You can understand why he wouldn't want to remain up there—he missed her. But you were settled, and to move you would have been hard on you, or any child barely three years old. We hired a lady to take care of you for a while and she slept on a cot in your room. Do you remember her?"

"No, I don't. My memory doesn't go back very far, I'm afraid."

"Well, she stayed less than a year, so it's no wonder. Anyway, Maud came then, and looked after you. As well as the rest of us. You could go up and down those stairs like a kitten so we felt you were as safe there, or safer, than you'd have been on the second floor."

"Is it all right if I move now?"

"Of course it is, child, you know that. I feel like one monkey in a barrel anyway, with your dad away so much and Lance never here at all, and all these empty rooms. But you'd better get your rest now." She yawned, and Ellen smiled to herself and leaned over to kiss the aged cheek.

"Good night, Granny."

"Ummm. It's nearly morning."

"Good morning then."

She slid off the bed and ran out of the room, closing the door softly behind her.

Though she took a blanket and went downstairs to a sofa, she sat wide awake until dawn. Some activity from the barns reached her ears. A voice once, laughing, that sounded like the ranch manager, Rodney Jarvis. Excitement quickened her heart. She had developed a schoolgirl crush on him when he came to manage the Crayley ranch five years ago. Her years away at school evidently hadn't completely cured her. The sound of the jeep came then as it roared away north. Rodney probably going to see about cattle. For a moment Ellen's thoughts followed the jeep and its good-looking driver. How lovely it would be for her to be riding along in the early October dawn, the cool wind blowing in her face. She knew now why she had been more than glad to come home, why the ranch seemed to her the most exciting place in the world.

But then the sound of the jeep was gone, and her thoughts went back to her third floor bedroom, and the dream that was so realistic it was more like a memory than a dream. The girl was nine or ten years old, she was sure of that. But the hate and malevolence in that diamond-shaped face was as old as Satan. Once, years ago, when she had run screaming from the nightmare, sobbing out in Granny's arms, "Sh-she wants to k-kill me, Granny ..." her grandmother held her back, arm's length, and looked into her face and demanded, "What does this girl look like, Ellen? Tell me!" So Ellen described her. Teeth that gleamed, black hair covering her cheeks. And as she talked she watched Granny's face turn pale. "Who is she, Granny?" she asked, but Granny only hugged her tight in her warm arms and said, "Hush, baby, she's no one. She's only a bad dream."

Ellen remembered now, and felt the same uneasiness. As if, for a moment, even Granny saw the girl and knew her, and thereby made her real. A girl with hate and evil so fierce that it someday would reach her, a girl who lived among the shadows of the vacant rooms on the third floor and came at night into her bedroom to watch her from the foot of the bed.

"That's ridiculous," Ellen said softly aloud and stood up, shaking her robe down. She folded the blanket and carried it under her arm as she went into the kitchen.

Coming through the back door was George Miller, ancient fixture of the ranch, his face almost as lined as Granny's. He carried a coal bucket in each hand. Ellen hurried to hold the door for him.

"Good morning, Mr. Miller." Everyone else called him George, but Granny's sense of propriety insisted that Ellen address him formally. He always returned the compliment.

"And good morning to you, Miss Ellen. Right chilly out this morning. Are you ready for fires?"

"Yes, sir." She smiled. "It's right chilly in, too.'"

Behind her came the squeaking irritation of Miss Maud's voice "... heating an old house like this with nothing but stoves and a few fireplaces and the ceilings twenty feet high is impossible and I haven't stopped shaking since I came here twenty years ago."

Ellen corrected her gently. "Sixteen years ago, Miss Maud." The ceiling height was an exaggeration too, but Ellen let that slide by.

"Seems like forty ..." Miss Maud said. "If a body ever caught pneumonia in this house, he'd die; no doubt about that ..."

There was more. From Miss Maud there was always more. But the sound was lost under the racket George Miller made pouring coal into the cookstove firebox. Ellen looked from one face to the other, her amusement growing. The old man wore a faint smirk of satisfaction as if he delighted in making enough racket to drown Miss Maud's shrill whine, but Miss Maud went right on talking, her lips moving soundlessly. Her bony hands clutched each bony elbow as if to warm them, and her eyes followed the movement of each chunk of coal into the firebox.

The bucket was nearly empty then and Miss Maud's voice filled the sudden quiet.

"... saw them leave, I sure didn't sleep much last night. You'd better take that other bucket up to Louise and start a fire. Lord only knows how she can stand ..." George Miller interrupted to ask Ellen, "You got any matches?"

Without pausing, Miss Maud changed subjects and answered him. "I took a new box up to Louise's room last night because it looked to me like it might frost and I wouldn't be surprised if the water froze and the pipes all burst ..."

George muttered, "It didn't get down to freezing."

"... that's all I need is burst pipes so I'd have to carry water then from a windmill somewhere in a cow pasture ..."

Ellen led the way into the back stairwell, closing the door on Miss Maud's voice. She could hear it yet, though only an indistinguishable murmur because Miss Maud always lowered her voice when she was alone.

"My god," George said, as he had innumerable times in the past, "don't that woman ever shut up?"

Ellen laughed. "Miss Maud is nervous. That's the way she relieves her anxieties. She doesn't

mean to annoy people."

"I'm glad I live in the bunkhouse. If I had to listen to her all day, I'd have anxieties too."

Ellen went ahead of him up the stairs. "Did Rodney go to the north range?"

"Yeah. Took a couple of boys up to mend fence. It takes a cold morning like this to make a feller glad he's retired, so he don't have to do nothing but build fires."

Ellen couldn't even have said how long George Miller had worked on the Crayley ranch. She knew when he reached the age of sixty-five because it had been a family item of interest. At her own age of eleven she had thought it the great passover, something like crossing the Great Divide in the mountains she could see from her bedroom window, while the rest of the family watched to see what George was going to do. For years he had looked forward to being sixty-five so he could retire. It turned out to be nothing but a birthday because he decided to stay on, if the Crayleys didn't mind, because he had no family, and nowhere else to go. Since then he had done more or less as he wished, and had taken the fire-building chores on himself.

Granny was sitting up in bed, ready for them, and Ellen left them carrying on their usual conversation while Mr. Miller built a fire in the small fireplace.

The second floor had two bathrooms, tucked into what had formerly been one small bedroom, and they both were heated by very modern electric ceiling heaters. Ellen stripped and stood for a moment in the glow of the heater before she stepped into the shower stall. All her clothes were upstairs. The bath had been on impulse, a way of ridding herself of a bad night. She wrapped the robe around her slightly damp body and ran up the steep, narrow stairs at the end of the hall, and into her room on the third floor.

The shadows were still there, still alive, behind heavy furniture. As she dressed she wondered which of the other two rooms had belonged to her mother. In all her years of thinking about a mother she couldn't remember, a mother whose face was a photograph on her dresser, she had simply placed her in the room downstairs with her dad. To know that once she was here, across the hall, or at the end of the hall, gave her a queer feeling of unease.

She stood still, frowning at her reflection in the mirror, wondering why it had suddenly affected her that way. Afraid of her own mother? How silly. She smiled at herself, saw that her dark hair had fallen out of the barrette that held it back from her forehead, and picked up a brush to redo it. With her hair forward over her cheeks, her face was a narrow oval, not a diamond. But if her chin had been a bit more pointed, and her forehead higher and more peaked ... She turned away from her reflection. Of all things, she didn't want to see the nightmare girl in her own mirror.

After breakfast, after part of the house was warm and Granny was helped down the long stairs, Ellen went back up to choose a new room. Granny had suggested the one across the hall from her own room, but the view from the window was flat and dreary, eastward, toward the town and away from the mountains. She wanted to change rooms, not views. The great range of the Rockies rose westward, and Ellen finally found the room with the same view as her own. It was at the end of the hall where the third story stairway opened nearby. A bit of minor deductions convinced Ellen it was the room beneath her old room.

She began by making the bed and bringing down from upstairs her own heavy bedspread of ivory lace. An ancestor had tatted it and she treated it like the antique it was. When the bed was made she prepared to move the family photographs. Uncle Lance, framed, looking very much like a riverboat gambler with not a practical brain in his head. Her own father, several years his brother's senior, the kind of serious face no one would ever notice twice. And her mother. Blonde, blue-eyed, pretty. Ellen had often tried to find herself in that picture and failed. She decided if she resembled any of the family, it was her rather dark and reckless Uncle Lance. Compared to her own black hair and eyes and olive complexion though, he looked quite fair.

An unexpected knock on the door caused her to nearly drop the photograph. She whirled to see George Miller standing in the doorway. "Sorry, Miss Ellen," he said. "I didn't mean to startle you. I thought maybe you'd a' heard me coming up the stairs with these clompers of mine."

"Oh—I guess I wasn't listening."

"Miss Louise said you was a' moving and might need some help."

"I don't think so, Mr. Miller; thanks anyway. I'm in no hurry. I'm just taking my clothes and all the keepsakes down. If it takes me a month, it doesn't matter."

"Well then ..." He had started to move away, but his eyes found the heavy frames of the pictures and he paused. "I could carry them for you since I'm here."

"Thank you. If you don't mind."

"No trouble. Just lay them here on my arms. Who's the pretty girl?"

Ellen felt pleased, and tilted the picture so that he could see it more clearly. "That's my mother."

"Your *mother*!" His voice exploded with surprise, and Ellen looked quickly up into his face.

"Why yes. Why?"

The frown was deep above his eyes as he stared at the picture. "Who told you that was your mother?"

"I—I don't know." His tone left her confused suddenly. "Everyone. I mean I've just always known it was. Why? What's wrong?"

Gradually, in a time that seemed long to Ellen, his face cleared. And then he said, "I guess I just forgot what she looked like. I can see now that's her."

"You knew her? I'd forgotten you lived here when she was here."

"Oh yes. I was here then. And long before. But I was out on the range a lot in them days."

"Did you know her very well?" Ellen couldn't keep the eagerness from bubbling out. "Granny and Dad just won't talk about her much. I guess they got tired of my questions."

"Like I said, I was out on the range a lot. Only knew her to speak to." He was turning away, going toward the stairs. "Where do you want these put?"

"I'll show you. She was so young, you know. And died in an accident. Automobile."

"Was that what it was?"

Ellen went down the stairs sideways, looking back up at his face, her hand on the smooth railing against the wall. "It was such a sudden thing. She'd gone to visit an old aunt, her only relative. Isn't that sad? She never got there. And then the aunt died."

"So she don't have no living relations left?"

"No, no one but me. Were you at her funeral? You must have been since it was right here."

"No. I was up on north range, herding cattle."

They had reached the other room and he laid the pictures on the antique lace spread before Ellen could stop him. Then, while she carefully removed them, he disappeared with a brief good-bye as if he had suddenly remembered another job he had forgotten to do.

"Oh well," Ellen said to the bedspread when she saw no harm had been done. "How is he to know you're old?"

The October wind screamed under the roof above the one tall window in her new room. She pushed at the draperies to let in more light, and saw that a heavy cover of clouds was responsible for the growing dark. An occasional drop of rain streaked across her window pane, and the mountains, usually so close and so huge, were completely blocked out by the dark mist of the clouds.

"There'll be snow on the mountains tomorrow," she said gaily to the room in general, thinking she was getting as bad as Miss Maud to go on talking whether anyone was there or not. "Rain here, evidently. I wonder if Rodney is back?" Her voice sobered and softened, and then was silent as her eyes searched the barns and the area around the bunkhouse for the jeep. When she finally found it, nearly hidden in the machine shed, she smiled slightly and drew back. She hadn't admitted it for a long time, and barely let herself think of it, but she liked knowing that Rodney was around. The rain by then had nearly obscured the landscape.

They were at dinner that evening, the rain still closing them in, when the phone rang. Miss Maud, who always ate with the family, got up to answer it. In a moment she called back for Louise. Her stringy voice came through from the kitchen, "It's Lance, Louise, and he says he's got great news for you but he doesn't say what."

Ellen watched the light flash on her grandmother's face. She sat up straighter, her small body suddenly not so bent with arthritis.

"Lance," she repeated, breaking into Maud's information. "News?" And then to hide her pleasure as she got up from her chair, "To hear from Lance at all is news." She put out her hand for support and Ellen helped her to the telephone in the kitchen and remained beside her though she yearned to run to the other end of the house to her father's office where the only other phone was located.

Granny was saying, while for once Maud was still, "What? *What?*" And then, "I'm so glad, Lance. When can we meet her?"

Ellen and Miss Maud exchanged glances and Miss Maud's eyebrows raised to nearly touch her hair. "*Another* woman ..." she whispered shrilly. "How many does this make you reckon?"

And Granny finished with, "We'll be looking for you." And said triumphantly to Maud as she replaced the receiver, "This time he's married!"

Miss Maud snorted. "What does that count these days—he'll probably be divorced before you know it and ..."

"No, I don't think so. You didn't hear him talk about her." She put her hand on Ellen's arm. "Let's go back to the table, dear."

"Well it's time he's getting a wife ..." Miss Maud was saying as she followed along. "What is he now thirty-six? I wonder how old the bride is—about eighteen probably—that's the age most men ..."

"He didn't say how old she is. But we'll know soon enough. He was calling from somewhere in Nevada and said they would be here for dinner tomorrow night."

When they were seated again Granny repeated the conversation word by word, and the next hour was spent discussing it.

When the house was quiet, except for the wind and the rain and a rather curious bell that rang somewhere far away in the night, when all had retired and Ellen sat in her new bed, a magazine on her knees, the conversation continued through her mind. "She's great, Mother, you'll love her." And her grandmother's softly spoken wish, "Maybe there'll be a little one someday soon, before I'm gone."

Ellen couldn't concentrate on her magazine. Uncle Lance was coming home. Breezing through, as he used to say? She couldn't remember a time when he had spent more than two weeks at home. Her grandmother thought the new wife would settle him down, but Ellen wondered.

What kind of woman had Lance chosen? Or, what kind of woman had finally caught old breezing-through Uncle Lance?

The next day was full of activity, of getting ready for the long-absent son and his new bride. They made ready Lance's old room, and then Ellen spent the afternoon in the kitchen cooking. Granny wanted a feast prepared, so Ellen sent for a ham.

Although George Miller went after it, Rodney Jarvis delivered it. And Ellen found with embarrassment that her cheeks turned as hot as they used to when she was fifteen and he, new on the ranch then, a handsome twenty-two year old fresh out of college, had turned those squinting dark eyes that always seemed to be laughing in her direction. She had hoped to return home more sophisticated, at least enough to be able to speak to him without fainting.

"Good to have you home again, Ellen," he said smiling, but his eyes laughing as always as if he had just heard a joke he thought it better to ignore. He looked for a moment, after he placed the ham carefully on the counter, as if he were going to reach over and pull one of her long braids. Just a few years ago, that simple action had almost sent her into ecstasies. His sleeves, rolled high, showed brown skin and strong muscles.

Just as always she wondered how those arms would feel, and just as always she stammered when she tried to talk to him. "G-good to be back, Rodney, thank you."

She was self-consciously aware of the big apron she wore and the spots of flour on it, and she wondered how untidy her hair must look since it was no longer in braids. She had smoothed it back with her hands and tied a scarf around the rope it made on her shoulders, all without ever glancing in a mirror. But if Rodney thought she was homely or beautiful, he didn't let on. His dark eyes were laughing and teasing. No more.

"George said you wanted a ham. Said you had company coming."

"Yes," she said, going from stammers to breathlessness. "Uncle Lance. And his wife. But you've never met Uncle Lance, have you? I think you came to work on the ranch a month or two after Uncle Lance last came home."

"No, I never met him." He came closer, looking down at her, smiling less.

She turned and pretended to examine the ham so that she could breathe. The effect he had on her was—almost humiliating. "He, Uncle Lance, is a lot younger than my father. He's only about sixteen years older than I am. That's quite a lot but—I mean it's not like Dad's thirty-two years, you know." She bit her lips and faced him, looking squarely into his eyes. "Granny spaced her sons quite far apart. But Uncle Lance uh, has never been married before. Thank you for bringing the ham, Rodney. You must come in for dinner and meet the rest of the family."

"Thanks, but some other time, maybe. I'm on my way to the foothills now to see if that new covering of snow here caught any new calves. See you."

She watched him walk away, watched the motion of his square shoulders as he went down the path, and felt the rise of a yearning both sweet and sad grow in her. She watched him leap into the jeep like a man mounting a horse, and spin away toward the mountains. Then she turned back to her work, taking particular care, wondering how she could question Mr. Miller on Rodney's favorite foods without seeming suspicions.

She recalled in mortification how she used to follow Mr. Miller around, when Rodney wasn't available, questioning him on every aspect of Rodney, from the names of the women he dated to the name of the soap he used. Even George Miller had laughed at her; no wonder Rodney did. Though he obviously had tried to conceal his amusement. And probably he spent a lot of effort trying to keep out of her reach.

She wondered how a man felt to be so adored by a young girl. Every time he went out with a new woman, she had kept her fingers crossed hoping he wouldn't get married. It had evidently worked.

At twenty-seven he was more attractive than ever—and still a bachelor.

Granny's old-fashioned teachings had influenced her more than her three years away at college plus the many mod friends she'd met, known and finally left again. She'd never want Rodney to know now how she felt until first he came to her.

Miss Maud's voice came along the hall, trailed by the lady in person. "... be sick if she doesn't watch out with so much excitement I think he should at least have written ahead and mentioned the girl instead of just springing her on his mother all at once like that it doesn't show much con ..."

"Granny seems to be taking it very well," Ellen said, interrupting, as one always had to do in order to get anything said to Miss Maud. "She's delighted, in fact."

"... sideration. Well, yes, she is. She thinks she wants more grand-babies. Humph, that's all I need—diapers to wash—the way my back is ..."

"I'm sure no one would expect you to wash diapers, Miss Maud. Even if they stayed here. Which is not likely. They're only coming to visit."

"I don't need to be doing any wash at all."

"I'll do the wash, Miss Maud, while I'm here."

"No, no, that's my job and—while you're here? You're not leaving again? Didn't you get through with that school?"

"Not quite. Of course I brought my books along and can do some off-campus work. I may not go back until spring."

"Then I don't know what you'd be thinking of leaving for. You're supposed to stay with your grandmother while she needs you and she does, what with everyone else gone all the time. Now me—I'm not much good ..."

"You're worth your weight in gold, Miss Maud."

"... but I do the best I can. Oh pouf, Ellen. You flatter a body."

Through the rest of the afternoon Ellen divided her attention to the cooking, thinking of Rodney, wondering what Lance's wife would be like—what kind of woman it had taken to throw a freedom-loving man like Lance Crayley, and snatches of the talk that rolled endlessly from Miss Maud's mouth.

Late in the afternoon when most of the dinner was ready and she could turn it over to Miss Maud to finish and serve, Ellen went upstairs to dress. She had in mind to wear new evening pants she had bought in Denver and found she had forgotten that most of her clothes were still in the third story bedroom.

The house upstairs was cold and silent. The wind had settled enough so there was only an occasional whine as it felt its way around sharp corners. Downstairs Granny's voice called, sounding far away, instructing Maud to fetch George now and get the fires going. Granny had been taught to be conservative with fuel because, in her father's day, fuel in this prairie land was more precious than money. Ellen rubbed the goose-bumps on her arms and wondered how Uncle Lance's bride would like it here—the cold, the wind, the scarcely modern antique house. Oh well, she thought then, they probably wouldn't stay long enough to form many opinions. Although Ellen rather wished they would. It would be nice to have other young people in the house, and especially another girl. Someone she could talk with and be friends with.

She went to the stairs that curved out of sight into the third story and looked up. The falling dusk had already plunged the stairs into near dark. Switching on the light helped only a little because it was one bulb far up on the ceiling of the third floor, above the drop into the walled stairwell. She hesitated going up, feeling a nervousness that puzzled her considering the years she had lived up there without a second thought. She almost decided to wear something else. But then she made up her mind that nothing but the pants would do and ran up the stairs without pausing, the way she always had.

Once out into the lighter, large hallway, she relaxed. Though the goosebumps came again to the backs of her arms, she went into her old room without giving in to the temptation to look over her shoulder. Strange, that since she had come home it seemed something, an unseen presence, was invading the third story. Or perhaps had invaded it while she was gone. Of course it could simply be the return of the dream that gave her the feeling of being watched all the time.

She went immediately to the window and looked out. The sun had dropped low behind the mountains, leaving in the thinning clouds brilliant reds and golds. The jeep was still gone, but the bunkhouse lights were on and smoke trailed straight up from the chimney. She hoped Rodney came in before much later. The soft new snow in the foothills could be treacherous.

Ellen brought several dresses from her closet along with robes and pant-suits and started out of the room when it came to her mind again that her mother had lived in one of the other rooms. She stopped, feeling oddly that she was deserting her, that her mother didn't want her to go. Her eyes went from one closed door to the other, one across the hall, one at the end of the hall. Then, on impulse, she dropped the clothes over a chair in the hallway and went to the room that joined her own, opened the door and ran her hand over the wall to find the antique button switch. The room was even darker than her own though it had three tall, narrow windows instead of one as in her room. The windows were covered with heavy lace curtains that filtered almost all light.

The button switch didn't have any effect on the darkness. Ellen looked up at the ancient ceiling fixture and saw that the bulb sockets were empty. She didn't go on into the room. It smelled as though it had never been heated or opened to outside air, and in her memory it had not. It had not occurred to her to search any room for anything that might have belonged to her mother, and if there was anything here it wasn't out in sight. The bed was huge and heavy, similar to her grandmother's bed, and the other furniture—dressers, chests, tables, chairs, more than really was necessary for a bedroom—was of the same dark, heavy, ornately-carved wood that furnished the rest of the house. The carpet was floral, big roses on a dark background. There was no sign of anyone ever having lived in this room, and perhaps no one had.

She moved back, closing the door, saying in a whisper, "I'll have to ask Granny which room it was." Then she ran down the stairs and paused just long enough to switch out the light.

WITHIN THE HOUR she was ready. The soft material whispered against her thighs as she went along the hall. All the lights were on, and there was in the air a faint smell of coal smoke. Uncle Lance's old room had a welcoming open door for the first time in five years. Ellen could hear George Miller's coal bucket rattling as he dumped more coal on the fire in Lance's room. Her own room would be next, she supposed. It had in one corner a tiny black pot-bellied stove sitting on a hearth of bricks, and a slender, black pipe running up and into a chimney in the wall. Compared to what she'd had upstairs, no heat source at all, she was now in the so-called lap of luxury.

She tied the sash around her twenty-three-inch waist and went down the stairs.

Granny, dressed in navy blue, wearing the sapphire necklace that came out of her private safe only a few times in a decade, was in the dining room instructing Miss Maud about the table. And Miss Maud was replying. And replying.

"... if I'd known there'd be such a fuss about all this, I'd have spoken to my nephew about visiting him and his wife ...", Miss Maud was saying, "... all this fancying up makes me so fidgety I could pull my hair. I never claimed to be a—a—nothing but a plain and common cook and up until now it was good enough ..."

"A bit more to the right, Maud," Louise Crayley said, waving a hand at a glass.

Ellen bent and kissed her grandmother's cheek quickly. "How pretty you look, Granny."

"It was good enough it's not like we lived in the middle of high society don't you reckon Lance would have told her it's a cattle ranch and no city here just a cattle town ..."

"That doesn't mean we can't use our good crystal, Maud. Thank you, dear. Of course *you're* always pretty. Never need makeup or jewelry. Never even need to pinch your cheeks the way I use to. "

"... dusty and windy and yes she is isn't she? I always thought she must look like her poor young mother because she sure doesn't take after the Crayleys ..."

Granny's voice was suddenly sharper than Ellen had ever heard. "Lance is quite dark, too. Ellen's mother was fair."

Ellen saw Miss Maud draw a deep breath, and she hurriedly filled the moment of silence the breath required: "Granny, which room did you say Mother had?"

Louise Crayley's veiled, colorless eyes stared for a moment at Ellen, and Ellen had to hurry on to explain, for already Miss Maud's mumbles were gathering force. "When I went up to get my clothes I —well I wondered. I thought it would be nice to know."

"Your mother's room," Granny's eyes wandered away as in a dream. "Yes. I believe it was the one on the south. It's been so long now. It might be better if you asked your daddy when he gets back."

A door slammed somewhere in the house and a voice that sounded only vaguely familiar called out, "Mother! Maudie!"

Confusion took over then. Miss Maud was practically turning circles and Granny seemed years younger in her movements as she went forward with outstretched arms. Ellen was aware of the masculine voice, the narrow, tanned face that wasn't as dark as she remembered, of herself standing back and looking on like a stranger in her own home. And of the girl who stood in the doorway behind Lance.

Ellen stared at the girl. Young, strikingly tanned, with hair so pale it gave unreal contrast. A faint smile was on her lips as her eyes left

Lance and his mother and Miss Maud and swiftly took in the table and the room.

And then came to light on Ellen. Cold chills, one after the other, traveled in silent warning up Ellen's spine.

Lance was turning to her then. "Is this that beautiful little niece of mine?" One rather soft hand took her wrist and pulled her into his arms. He kissed her, and turned with one arm still around her waist. "Here she is. Ellen, Mother, Maudie, meet my childbride. Tina was hoping you'd be here, Ellen. I thought you were living in Denver now."

"No. I was there only for school. That's nearly over now."

Ellen felt forced to smile. She held out her hand to the girl Uncle Lance had called his childbride. With the shivers running over her arms and the back of her neck, raising in her a nearly overpowering desire to hold both hands safely behind her. To never, never let the girl touch her.

The girl's steps forward seemed to last forever. Then the ice cold fingers touched Ellen's, and she couldn't control the sudden tremble.

Tina Crayley laughed softly and said, "My cold hands shocked you? I'm not used to such weather, I'm afraid. But I'm so glad to meet you, Ellen. So glad you're here."

Ellen felt her own smile waver and fade. She didn't answer because her voice had failed her. She was glad when the moment passed and Tina turned to the others. Turned away from her the dark gleaming eyes and the diamond face of the nightmare girl.

## CHAPTER 2

Through the long evening while the clock's hands scarcely
moved at all, while there was no way in the world to get
herself politely excused from the group, Ellen avoided meeting Tina's
eyes directly. Even when she was drawn into the conversation by a
question, she kept her own eyes averted.

Uncle Lance finally said, "Is it my imagination, or is Ellen pale?"

Her grandmother looked at her. "Aren't you well, dear?"

Ellen grabbed at the chance to make something of it and get away,
as Miss Maud had done after dinner. "I am tired. Perhaps I should
say goodnight."

Lance broke in agreeably. "That's a good idea for both you girls.
Tina's had a long day too. Why don't you go up together? And
Mother and I will make up for lost time, here."

From the corner of her eyes Ellen could see Tina looking at her,
leaning forward, and the thought of walking alone in the silent dark
above with that girl took more courage than she had. "No," she said
quickly, groping for an excuse again. But it was too late. Tina had
risen and was looking down at her, smiling.

"I would like that," Tina said. "I doubt if I could find our room again without help. And I know Mother Crayley would like to have Lance to herself for a while." Tina leaned down and kissed both of them and then put her hand out to Ellen, the smile still there, the eyes sparkling with demons unseen by the others.

In order to avoid making a fool of herself, Ellen pretended not to see the cold hand reaching to her. She too got up and kissed the cheeks of both Granny and Uncle Lance. Then she went toward the large central hall and the wide stairway at the front that rose to branch into the divided hall of the dimly lighted second floor. She forced a conversation of sorts, a type of chatter that sounded to her own ears like something from Miss Maud.

"I suppose the house does seem rather strange and large and easy to be lost in to someone not used to it. I found Denver that way when I first went there, but after a while I began to know it. Of course you really wouldn't get lost here—there aren't as many bedrooms as it seems. Only eleven on this floor, and ..."

The soft, fine voice broke through. "I believe I saw a third story? Rather like a small box on top a large hat. An addition maybe?"

"No, not an addition. At least not that I ever heard. I don't know why it was built in such an awkward way. I think the first owner, also a Crayley, lived up there where he could have a good view of most of the ranch—that is, as far as he could see. It's a very tall house, the ceilings so high and all."

"I saw windows. Isn't it an attic?"

"Oh no." Ellen could feel the eyes, and somewhere beneath the softness of the voice a kind of laughter that didn't fit the question. She said, "There are three bedrooms." And then she was quiet because she was wondering how those windows had been visible in the dark. How, even, the odd shape of the upper part of the house had been visible. Against the sky, maybe. They walked down the hall, their steps only slightly muffled on the carpets that had not been changed in Ellen's lifetime, nor her father's. Beside her the soft voice was making conversation again.

"So many doors. It really is a very large house, and a bit creepy if you don't mind my saying so. When I found out Lance was eager to come home to live I was really worried—you know, nothing but two old ladies, and a much older brother-in-law who is seldom home. I can't say how pleased I was to see you, really. You know, to have someone my own age seemed too good to be true. I love your gran already, and that dear nervous lady, what do you call her? Miss Maudie?"

But Ellen was hearing mainly one statement, and she stopped, facing Tina where the light was most dim, not far from the bedroom door that stood open, waiting. "Home to live?"

"Why, yes." The narrow but full-cut palely painted lips smiled. The eyes were like dark holes in the diamond face. She stood close to Ellen, looking up slightly. "That is all right, isn't it?"

"I ..." Ellen had not noticed before that Tina was slightly shorter. Shorter and a bit plumper, her figure rounded and quite full. More mature? "Yes, of course it's all right. Grandmother will be pleased."

Tina turned, profile to Ellen, and began to walk slowly on. "I know that after awhile I'll love it here. We both want a large family, and this would be the ideal place to bring kids up, wouldn't it? How lucky you were to have such a nice home. That really puts you in a minority, you know? I wonder what percentage of kids in the world are so fortunate to live in a great ancestral home, and have all the money they want? Oh well. Perhaps now my kids will be in that minority." She paused by the open door and looked in without entering. "Oh, here it is. There's the lovely new luggage Lance so thoughtfully bought for me. But I'll bet I would never have found the right room if someone hadn't left everything where I could see it." Her laughter then, as she glanced back at Ellen, was almost a childlike giggle.

Ellen felt herself relaxing. Tina seemed a rather ordinary girl after all, in spite of the touch of bitterness she had, and seemed to be going out of her way in search of a friend. She made Ellen feel ashamed and selfish for not wanting her around, for finding in her, a flesh and blood person, the face of a girl in an old nightmare.

"Did they show you the bath?" Ellen asked, and was answered by a quick smile and a shake of the blonde head. "There're only two, and convenient to very few rooms. The towels are even worse to get to; they're down at the other end of the hall, near Granny's room, in the linen closet that divides that part of the hall. But I did remember to leave a couple extra in the bath for you." She pushed open a bathroom door. "The bath is warm now, too. And there's plenty of hot water. That's one thing we do always have plenty of."

"I'm sure I'll have time for a long bath before Lance comes up."

"This is the bath with the tub. The other has the shower."

"Would I be keeping someone else ...?"

"Oh no. No, you go ahead and spend as much time there as you'd like." Ellen could smile at last at the rather small face before her. "To save you a trip back down the hall, I'll bring your things if you want me to."

"I can get them. First, let me walk with you up to your room." Her eyes turned immediately to the dark, walled stairway to the third floor as if she had been there many times and knew it well.

Ellen said, in a voice that sounded hoarse to her ears, "My room is not up there."

The other girl whirled, staring at Ellen with eyes wide and as dark as her own. She seemed inordinately surprised, and when she spoke again she faltered slightly. "Then—but I thought—you said there were bedrooms up there."

"Yes."

Tina let out a breath, and smiled. "Oh, I remember now. How dumb of me. You said there are three bedrooms up there, that was all you said. I don't know where I got the impression—I guess Lance told me. I'm sorry, Ellen. Did I say something wrong?"

"Of course not. Why do you think that?"

"Oh because of the way you sounded, and the way you looked.

Really quite scared." The word ended on a soft, girlish giggle, and once again she looked at the dark stairs. "I'm glad you don't sleep up there. You don't happen to have any ghosts, do you?"

"No." Ellen returned her smile. "If so they're very quiet."

"If you did, I could see why the mere mention of a bedroom up there would turn you pale. It rather turns me pale anyway, just looking at those creepy stairs."

Ellen tried to relax again and accept Tina's offer to accompany her upstairs for what it was—an understandable error, or Uncle Lance's information. But she couldn't. Her feeling of foreboding had returned and it was all she could do to keep from running downstairs, away, anywhere away. There was something about Tina, a cunning masquerade, or a hypocrisy, that reached Ellen's senses like the boring of a caterpillar. "If you'll excuse me I think I'll go on to bed," Ellen murmured.

"Of course. I didn't mean to keep you standing."

Tina stood watching her, and Ellen wished that she would go back to her own room. But when Ellen told her goodnight and walked away, Tina was still watching. Ellen felt the eyes following her, and in her doorway she almost gave in and looked back. But she was afraid of what she would see. A small, diamond face with gleaming eyes and teeth, a horrible smile, black hair falling straight down each cheek, and hands raised over her head and shaped into claws ...

Ellen closed the door and leaned against it, heart pounding, eyes closed. The room was dark as an underground tunnel, but she didn't care. At least she was alone. If only she had someone she could talk to about her ridiculous fear. Lance's young wife the girl in her nightmares? She had never seen her before in her life, yet she couldn't seem to help her feelings.

Maybe tomorrow it would be different. She was tired from a long day's work. All she needed was sleep and rest.

She felt her way across the room to a lamp and pushed the

button. The light was comforting. Warmth came from the little iron stove. She went to the chair beside it and sat for several long minutes staring at the little door, listening to the murmur of the fire.

The wind had stopped with only an occasional gust that whined mournfully under the eaves. Ellen heard the faint ting of a bell so far, far away, and she began to listen, carefully, straining to hear, to place it, define it, recognize it. She recalled hearing it a night or two ago when the wind had blown hard and strong, yet the bell had been as penetrating then as now. She began to run through her mind the things it could be, and to discard them as soon as they occurred to her. Church bells in a faraway village? No. Someone ringing the school bell in one of the haunted little one room schools that were no longer used? No. It was a finer-toned bell than those. Much finer.

She got up suddenly and went to the window and pushed the sash up. The storm window hadn't been hung yet, so there was only the screen between her and the night air. For a moment the bell seemed to have gone but then she heard it again, still faint and far away. She leaned close to the screen and listened and suddenly it seemed to be coming from above, from the top floor of the house. Or somewhere above.

Ellen drew back quickly, closed the sash and jerked the heavy draperies together. She listened, holding her breath, but all she heard was a sudden whine of the wind.

After a moment she drew a deep breath and busied herself, getting ready for bed. She hummed under her breath as she creamed her face, as she changed to pajamas. And she left the light on when she got into bed. It was a small, dark-shaded lamp, with a light soft and soothing. Cuddled down under soft blankets, her knees drawn up, her eyes found the ceiling and she shivered comfortably. At last she felt safe and warm. She wondered how she had survived sleeping alone on the third story for all those years.

When she awoke the room was cold, and the lamp looked sick in the daylight that managed to penetrate the draperies. The clock on the bed table told her she'd have to cook her own breakfast because Miss Maud was a stickler for early breakfasts, and clean kitchens. She would probably have the kitchen slippery clean by now.

In the hall outside her door she saw a bucket of coal George Miller had left, but she flung her door back and ran to take a shower and dress in the warmth of the bathroom. In pants and sweater she returned to her room only long enough to make the bed.

Downstairs she found Granny in the small sitting room reading the daily paper that reached them by special carrier every morning a day late. But they were used to it and Ellen would have thought nothing of it if she hadn't spent the past three years where people read the paper the same day it was printed. She didn't mention her thoughts though; she kissed the old lady's cheek and went on through the adjoining breakfast alcove into the kitchen.

"... too warm for much of a fire," Miss Maud was saying as she poked at the coals in the firebox of the stove with a long-handled fork. "But warm or not we have to have fuel when there's company for dinner ..."

"You could use the electric stove," Ellen said absently, shaking the coffee pot to see if someone had left a cup.

"... and supper too you know I never could cook on that high-falutin' electric stove; it gets too hot too fast and stays hot too long and food just doesn't taste as good, now me, I'll take iron between the fire and the pot—your Uncle Lance and Aunt Tina got up and ate at seven with the rest of us so where were you may I ask? Now they've gone on into town and I ..."

"I was wondering if they'd gotten up yet."

"... don't know when they'll be back mercy me, they were up before I was and as happy as two kids ..."

"I'd feel stupid calling her aunt as young as she is. I don't believe she's any older than I", Ellen said.

"... giggling and laughing and carrying on I'll fix you some cinnamon toast if you'd like Ellen ..."

"Oh I'd like, very much. Thank you, dear."

"Poof. I think I heard Lance tell your grandma that she's twenty-three but ..." Miss Maud paused and looked far off into the wall and for one moment was oddly silent. "... but it seemed to me when I looked at her this morning that she was a lot older than that." She sighed and began to move again, her quickness causing her to appear busier than she actually was, preparing toast, pouring coffee. "Never can tell how old a body is because some people age a lot faster than others; I guess now nobody would guess me to be only forty-six because I look like sixty-six but that's not the half of it—I feel like ninety-six."

Ellen resisted the urge to smile. And to remind Miss Maud that she'd been forty-six for twelve years that she could remember, and she didn't know how many years before that. But she did say, "And some people never age." But if Miss Maud heard her she didn't let it slow her down.

Granny came into the room leaning on her cane, moving slowly, dragging the foot that had been affected by a stroke she had survived years before when Ellen was a young teenager. She interrupted Miss Maud. "Did Maud tell you your uncle is considering living here? Tina wants to."

"Tina does? No, she didn't tell me that. She said Uncle Lance wanted to stay. Do you want toast, Granny?" She busied herself at the cabinet getting a small plate, pausing for her grandmother's answer, trying to hide her lack of enthusiasm. She felt selfish and hostile, traits she didn't like in anyone, but she couldn't help the sudden wish that Uncle Lance would decide to go on or back wherever he'd been spending his years.

"I've had breakfast, thank you." Granny sat down, slow and creaking as if each joint had to be pried loose, and at last comfortable, balanced her cane across her knees. A pleased look replaced the pained frown.

"Speaking of Tina—isn't she a lovely little thing? As cuddly as a doll, and so affectionate with Lance. No wonder he fell in love with her. Do you know what he calls her? His childbride, that's what. They've been married less than a week. She just couldn't wait to see the ranch, he said."

Miss Maud's mumbles rose. "... but there's something about her when she doesn't know anyone is looking at her when she isn't smiling—an *old* look about her ..."

"Nonsense!" Granny said in tempered sharpness as if nothing could daunt her good spirits, even criticism of her new daughter-in-law. "I think she has had a rather hard life. No home anymore. No relatives."

"What happened to them?" Ellen asked, bringing her plate and napkin to the table.

"I don't know. He just said she was orphaned when she was younger and has been on her own ever since."

"... a tightness around her mouth and hollows around her eyes ..."

Ellen said, "Do you think she'd be happy on the ranch? A city girl, I mean, would lose her mind here in the quiet of the country."

Granny replied, "She wants to live here. I think it's more her idea than Lance's. I've always hoped Lance would come home to live someday, and raise a family. And now she's brought him. She'll be happy. She wants to fill the house with children." The tucked-in smile and blissful light in Granny's eyes was as readable as the newspaper she carried in her left hand, forgotten.

Ellen said dryly, "Quite a feat."

Miss Maud interrupted her own muttered comments to emit a rare burst of laughter, and then she too dryly agreed. "Quite a feat is right and all I need is about ten pairs of feet running around overhead. I guess I'd better go out and get my own bucket of coal that George got in such a hurry to leave he didn't bring near enough to ..."

"Leave?" Granny said. "Where did he go?"

Miss Maud was on her way out the door and she didn't pause. " ...

well he sure didn't tell me but wherever it was it was enough to make him edgy like he had a burr under his ... "

The door slammed and the kitchen was quiet. Ellen and Granny looked at each other, both a bit startled at the depth of silence Miss Maud had left behind, and neither of them made an effort to break it for a few minutes. Then Granny spoke softly. "Well, anyway, they will be back for lunch. I wonder where George went?"

Ellen, wishing to know if Rodney were still around, said, "Perhaps I'd better go help Miss Maud with the coal." She got a coat from a downstairs closet and went out. Miss Maud was coming up the walk in a long, horsey stride, her head down against the wind, a bucket of coal in her hand, her lips closed. Ellen stepped aside. "Need some help, Miss Maud?"

"No I've already done all the damage I can do to myself I reckon —got coal dust up to my arm pit on one side and up to my shank on the other; some man ought to fix that place so's a woman could handle it or else keep enough ..."

She went on, talking, and Ellen turned toward the bunkhouse and the office. At least now she had an excuse for seeking out Rodney. She opened the door and found him, sleeves rolled high, behind the big, scarred desk that was a mess of papers and dirty coffee cups.

He looked up. "Well!" And leaned back slightly, looking at her.

She began gathering dirty cups. "Just like always," she said. "I'll bet these are the same papers that used to be here, and these are the same old dirty cups. Don't you have a dishwasher down here?"

"Yeah, but he took off this morning and went to town. Tell you what—in exchange for a little secretarial work, I'll wash the cups for you."

She glanced at him, laughing. "Some exchange that is! I'm not your *cup* washer."

"Hey now, you used to wash our cups."

"Yes, I remember. If ever there lived a sucker I was it. I think now you fellows stacked all your dirty dishes until you saw me coming."

He leaned back in his chair, his eyes teasing but observant. "After all these years away at school I think you deserve a promotion. To paper work. I sure could use a little help. How about it?"

"Okay. What do you want done?"

He leaned forward, scooped an armload of envelopes, papers, bills, and shoved them to one end of the desk. "They have to be categorized, set down, added up—oh nuts, you're the secretary, not me. You tell me what to do with them."

For two hours she worked with him, until everything was done and the desk was clean; and she thought as she worked that it was the greatest two hours she had ever spent. More thrilling than any date she had ever had. When his bare arm accidentally brushed hers it started a trembling within her that threatened never to stop.

"What I really came for," she said at last, "was to ask where Mr. Miller went. Granny wanted to know." Poor excuse. She was afraid to look at him.

"Shucks," he said lightly, "And all this time I've been thinking you came just to see me. What are you trying to do to my ego, anyway?"

"I think your ego was firmly made indestructible years ago. And nothing I could ever do or say would change that."

He laughed as if she had said something really funny, his eyes nearly closed, his gaze shadowed by lashes as thick and long as her own. She got up, feeling a bit chilled and uncomfortable under his laughter. A hotplate in the corner of the cluttered room held a large, dirty coffee pot. She checked and found it contained acid-strength coffee, enough for two short cups. She flicked on the burner. And then she waited, her arms folded.

The outside door suddenly crashed open, bringing wind, fine sand, an off-course tumbleweed, and George Miller.

"Goddamned wind tried its best to keep me from getting home."

He turned, stomping his feet in the doorway while the wind blew into the room the clods of drying mud and sand he dislodged.

"George, shut the damned door!" Rodney yelled over the racket.

George backed into the room and slammed the door, talking over his shoulder to Rodney. "I told you something was wrong, and I was right. There's no record of any death certificate in the Crayley County records ..."

He turned then and saw Ellen and his words stopped in mid-air. But the most startling thing to Ellen was how the color left his face. For a moment he looked sick. And Rodney, too, Ellen saw, had gone suddenly sober. But instead of looking at George Miller, his eyes were on her, as straight and as watchful as were the old man's. Ellen stepped forward after one dumbfounded moment and laid a hand on George's shoulder. Her voice was low with concern. "Are you all right, Mr. Miller?"

Rodney got up and patted George's back, his moment of silent seriousness gone. "Oh sure, George is all right, aren't you, George? Just swallowed a little air there, didn't you, George?" The old man nodded and Rodney's hand moved from George's back to Ellen's wrist and closed around it. "How about me walking you to the house? Miss Louise is going to be wondering first where her beautiful grand-daughter disappeared, and next thinking about firing me. It's too late in the season to find a new job. Come on."

He pulled her toward the door and out. She was so busy trying to protect her face from the blowing sand that she didn't even tell Mr. Miller goodbye. The door slammed again behind them and they went head-on into the wind. Rodney, talking above the wind, said, "I believe this is trying to blow us up some winter weather." Ellen didn't try to answer.

At the back door of the house, protected at last and able to raise her head, she brushed her black hair out of her eyes and smiled up at him. "Won't you come in and meet Uncle Lance? He'll be back for lunch."

"Thanks, but no. I met him this morning."

"Oh you did! I didn't know."

"You were probably still getting your beauty sleep. He's nothing at all like your daddy, is he?"

"No, but—no. Uh, did you meet ..."

After a moment he finished her sentence. "Aunt Tina? Isn't that what you call her?" His smile seemed more than teasing; it seemed mocking now, and Ellen felt an unreasonable dislike of the name. And the sharp pierce of another feeling that was close to jealousy.

"Do you know her so well?" she asked.

"Hey, do I detect a note of dislike there? Already?"

"Of course not. I only just met her myself. A person can't dislike someone they've just met, can they?" If she didn't admit it, maybe it would go away, she thought. And she would have to watch herself, if her feelings showed so plainly. "Come over then when you like," she said, a substitute for goodbye, and went on into the long, screened porch.

But this time she avoided the kitchen and took the door that brought her directly to the enclosed back stairs. At the foot of the stairs was a small windowless entry about ten feet square that contained the rising stairs, a door to the kitchen, a door to the central hall that reached the length of the house, and another door to a small dusty office that had belonged to the housekeeping staff in the days when so much household help was needed, when most of the rooms weren't closed off. Ellen had entered the room perhaps three times in her life. She knew it contained a large desk with many pigeon holes for bills and receipts, a few chairs, shelves on a wall to take the place of filing cabinets, and one narrow, heavily curtained window.

She would have passed its closed door without a thought had she not heard a movement, a rattle of paper. She paused, wondering who would be there in the cold, closed room, and then she shrugged and started into the stairwell. The door to the housekeeper's office opened suddenly, and Ellen glanced back to see Tina framed in the shadowed doorway. Tina stopped, obviously surprised, and stared at Ellen. For a long moment there was no smile on her lips, and her face in its diamond shape was hard and tense, her mouth pinched and tight, her eyes dark and secretive and as malevolent as the eyes in Ellen's dream.

Ellen took a step backwards, and bumped into the wall.

"Oh. Ellen," Tina said, smiling, sagging a bit as if in relief. "You nearly scared the socks off me, for a moment there you looked just like ..." She bit her lower lip and glanced over her shoulder. "I was exploring that—that incredibly stuffy place and was already half spooked. Then, when I opened the door and saw someone standing there so quietly, I nearly choked on my own heart. Say, you don't think we could have met somewhere before, do you?"

Ellen shook her head. "I don't think so. Probably not."

"You don't sound sure, though. What are you thinking of? Do I remind you of someone too?"

"No," Ellen said. Only Granny knew about her nightmares. She wouldn't dream of admitting such a thing to Tina. "No. I'm sure I've never seen you before. You remind me of no one."

"Well, you look like a woman I knew once. But I'll try not to hold that against you." Laughing, Tina closed the door and came to take Ellen's arm in hers, and together they climbed the narrow stairway, able barely to walk side by side. Tina told of her trip to town in tones girlish and trusting.

Ellen struggled to put aside her aversion and to be friendly. In a few days, she thought, I'll get used to her. I have to. For Granny's sake, for everybody's happiness, I have to. Near the door to her room Ellen stopped. "I came up to comb my hair, the wind is terrible."

Tina patted her own piled hair-do. "I noticed that. Of course I have to wear scarves when I go out. If I dared let my hair hang free, as you do, I wouldn't worry. I'd just let it blow."

"Dare?"

"Yes, well, I look awful that way."

"I'm sure you wouldn't. Would you like to come in with me?"

"Oh yes. Thank you."

Ellen could at least feel ashamed of her own feelings when she saw the pleasure her simple invitation gave Tina. She held the door and the girl went into the room and stood in the middle looking around.

"Of course I haven't lived here very long," Ellen said. "So it's just a room. I don't have all my things down yet from my old room."

Tina sat down on the bed and caressingly felt the bedspread. "How beautiful. Is it an heirloom?"

"Yes. It was tatted completely by someone far back in the family. A maiden aunt of Granny's."

Tina didn't answer. She seemed to be closely examining the bedspread, and Ellen waited for her comment. After a few moments Tina turned her attention to other things in the room. She walked slowly about, touching, running her fingers over anything within reach in the same caressing way. There was about her movements something that reminded Ellen of a silent cat, loving, rubbing soft fur against any object.

Tina saw the pictures then and went toward them, laughing, "Oh my gosh, don't tell me that's Lance. He was a handsome young thing, wasn't he? I like him better the way he is. Roughed up a bit. He looks too smooth and tender there." She pointed a finger at the photograph beside it. "Is that your father?"

"Yes. It's a rather recent picture."

"And who's this?"

"My mother."

The change in Tina's face was subtle, but unmistakable. She seemed frozen. She stared at the picture for a long while, saying nothing. Ellen wondered what she was thinking. "She died when I was very young," Ellen explained. "This is all I have. I don't remember her at all."

"Died," Tina repeated. Then, as if coming out of a dream, "My mother died too. But I remember her. Did your father give you this?"

"I don't remember that anyone gave it to me. I've always had it. Maybe mother gave it to me herself. I think it must be a graduation picture, don't you? She looks so young."

"I'm sure that's what it must be. A graduation picture." As Tina talked she moved toward the door. She smiled then and waved her hand. "Bye bye, see you later."

Slowly Ellen brushed her hair, thinking of Tina. Once she had seen the pictures she couldn't leave fast enough. Ellen paused, hairbrush dangling in her hand, and looked at the pretty, smiling face in the frame. Suddenly she was recalling George Miller's reaction to her mother's photograph. Strange. That might be understandable though, because he had known her, and probably he had created an image in his mind that was different from the photograph. But Tina?

George Miller entered her thoughts abruptly again, and for the first time since she left the ranch office she was hearing the words he had blustered in with—"I told you something was wrong, and I was right. There's no record of any death certificate in Crayley County ..." It couldn't have any connection with her mother. Her mother was buried on the hill!

Whatever he had been talking about evidently had not been intended for her ears. Ellen looked around slowly. Something was different at home now. There seemed a certain atmosphere around that was affecting everyone, something that was closing in, something that couldn't be stopped. And she felt like running, but she didn't know where to go. She couldn't leave Granny, and she didn't want to leave Rodney. Besides, this was her home. She went downstairs, determined to escape her gloomy feelings, but not succeeding.

The storm was increasing, wind screaming, driving the hard, tiny snowflakes like slivers of ice against the windows. No one was going out. Ellen was half glad and half sorry. She was glad that Uncle Lance was in the house, company for his childbride, and sorry that the storm was so fierce she couldn't sensibly walk down to the ranch office for an evening cup of coffee with Rodney. The snow came faster and thicker, shutting off the little light that usually entered the few windows in the old house. Miss Maud went muttering from room to room turning on lights.

Lance, relaxing in the favorite sitting room on a sofa beside Tina, his arms casually looped around her, laughed. "Miss Maudie is swearing, so help us!'"

"Nonsense!" said his mother. "Maud never swears." She raised her voice and called toward the hall, "Not too many lamps, Maud. There's no point in lighting rooms we don't use."

Ellen had been looking out a window, but she thought of the cold that came with the early storm and excused herself to go upstairs to add fuel to the little stove in her room.

Miss Maud was in the second floor hall, on her way back.

"... my house I'd sell it for junk and build a smaller one that I could keep warm and light though why there's any problem I don't know because there sure is no shortage of money, the Crayley's have always been rich ..."

"But maybe that's because they were always saving."

"They? Don't you consider yourself a Crayley? Well I put the light on at the far end of the main hall upstairs anyway, the one between your door and the two back stairs because I'd hate for George to trip and fall and he always brings the coal up the back you know, so we have to watch out for him, he may not be worth much but right now he's the only one willing to carry fuel and build fires and we ..."

She had gone on out of hearing, and Ellen went into her room.

The little stove huffed along, competing on its tiny scale with the sound of wind and snow-sleet on the windowpane. Someone had already filled it and returned the coal bucket, empty, to the hall beside her door. She closed the door, turned on a reading light near the stove and settled down in the armchair to read. Comfortable and relaxed, she had to admit it was rather cozy. Her earlier mood had finally changed. She decided she must be getting used to Tina and her startling resemblance to the little girl in her terrifying dreams.

Ellen didn't know how long she had been reading when the sound drew her mind away from the book. It was the bell again, faint, far away, and yet irritating, disturbing, as if part of its sound was pitched too high for her consciousness. Like an iceberg, only part could be heard, and the rest was there to crush her. She couldn't sit still. She lay the book face down on the footstool, got up and paced the floor a minute. Then she stopped to listen again.

So far away, and yet so close—ting-uh, ting-uh—a two syllable sound that was almost like a word spoken, or sung. She pressed both hands over her ears. She couldn't stand it. She felt in another moment she would scream. The wind blew hard, whistling a thousand tunes, but still the fine-toned bell permeated the atmosphere.

Ellen left her room and nearly ran the long, dim hallway to the front stairs, and down to the sitting room. The three were still there, almost as she had left them. She stopped, looking from one waiting face to the other. "Listen," she said. "Do any of you hear that bell?"

They listened, silent, waiting. But only the storm was there.

Tina spoke first, her voice high-pitched and childlike. "I don't hear any bell."

"I can't hear it either, now," Ellen said. "But it's about to drive me crazy. Upstairs it's very plain."

"I can't imagine what it could be," Granny said. "There's no bell here, anywhere, I'm sure."

"It isn't here," Ellen said. "It's somewhere far off. Why do you suppose it's ringing in this kind of weather? "

Lance pushed Tina over and sat up, grunting. "Let old Uncle see about it. Maybe it just sounds like a bell. Maybe it's the wind on the telephone wires."

Granny said, "There are no overhead wires anymore. They are in an underground cable."

"Oh-ho. Crayley County's gone uptown, huh? Well. Electric wires sing too, and I know they're still there. Come on, little niece, and we'll see."

He went ahead, Ellen and Tina following behind. When they reached her room they closed the door and listened, but now there was only the sound of the storm.

"Drat," Ellen said. "Of course it wouldn't ring when I want it to."

"It's only a part-time thing then," Lance said.

"Yes."

"Well, the next time you hear it, yell, and I'll see if I can track it down for you."

Ellen stayed after they had gone, listening, but there was no bell. After awhile she took a bath, dressed in warm pants and sweater and went downstairs to help Miss Maud with dinner.

"... come earlier every year I swear storming like this the sixteen of October what'll it be doing in another month? We won't be able to get out—what was it about a bell?"

"I don't know. I can't place it or think what it could be. Uncle Lance said it might be wind in the wires or something."

"Some farms over on the river still have those old dinner bells."

"Oh say, I never thought of that!"

"... and use them to call the men in from work ..."

"But on a snowy night like this?"

"... in the fields or the barns, they might be in the barns. I worked for a family once that had one of those big bells just beside the kitchen door and there was a rotten young boy that pulled it just to see me jump, you could hear one of those ring for miles ..."

Because Uncle Lance and Tina had taken the sofa where Ellen usually relaxed after dinner, she sat in a chair that gave her a view of Tina's profile, and she couldn't keep her attention from wandering there. The more she looked at Tina the more she had to admit her first impression was not merely a case of resemblance nerves. The resemblance was not only real, it was uncanny.

Ellen wanted to be alone, to think, to try to reason it out. Eventually it was bedtime, or at least late enough that she could politely leave the small gathering by the television.

She dressed in roomy, warm pajamas, and turned her electric blanket high. It wouldn't matter, she thought as she climbed into bed, if her small fire burned out and her room got cold. She wondered if Rodney had gone to bed yet. But she had come upstairs to analyze her nightmares, not daydream about Rodney Jarvis. She couldn't remember when the nightmares had begun, she had grown up with them. Every time she was ill, or had eaten too much, she had the nightmare. Nothing ever changed in it. The girl was there, at the foot of her bed and the face was the face of Tina Crayley.

Or could the answer be simply that the face could fit any dark-eyed girl with a pointed chin and high, narrow forehead—or any face of those general characteristics that might appear in this house. Of course that was the answer. It had to be. She couldn't have created in her dreams the child's face of a woman who would one day come to live in this house.

Satisfied with her reasoning she scooted down into bed, adjusted the blanket to a lower setting, reached over and turned out the bed lamp, and proceeded to think about Rodney. She drifted into sleep, her thoughts still pleasantly with him. She wondered dreamily if he ever thought about her.


ELLEN WOKE. The storm was still screaming at the side of the house, rattling something about the window, sounding as if it were tearing the shingles off the roof that sloped just above the window. Her room was dark and there was a feeling of inner stillness as if everyone but she slept soundly. She hadn't dreamed, but something had awakened her. For a moment she couldn't place it, and then, incredibly fine but piercing the noises of the storm, she heard it. Ting-uh—ting.

She sat up, pushing her blanket back, staring ahead into the dark room, her attention riveted. She was annoyed that the bell, so far away and so nearly inaudible, should bring her from a comfortable sleep. She reached for the light switch, and then got her robe and put it on. That much accomplished she stood in the middle of the room determined to find out where it came from and put an end to it if she could. She turned slowly, listening, and after awhile discovered the bell seemed slightly more audible near her door. She opened it and stepped into the long hall that was only dimly lighted by the small bulb at the end. She thought of doing as Uncle Lance had suggested and call him to help her, but decided not to waken him.

The storm was less noticeable in the hall, and in the heavy silence the bell too seemed to have gone; but then as she started to return to her room, she heard it again. The sound was sharply clearer, and it seemed to her that it was somewhere in the house. With a feeling of triumph she moved along the hall, slowly, guided by the faint ting-uh of the bell. She didn't really notice where it was leading until she reached the end of the hall. There was only the pale, shadowed light overhead, and the dark open stairwell into the third story.

She stepped up, one step, two, and as the bell became more clear she remembered that she first had heard it when she was still in her old room. But now the sound of it was changing and became teen-a, teen-a. Tin-a, Tin-a. Ellen stood still, staring up into the darkness, fear holding her and seeping through her as insidiously as the sound of the bell. And it sang in clear, flute tones on and on, Tin-a, Tin-a, Tin-a ...

It ended suddenly with the breaking of glass, a loud crashing and falling and shattering, as if several windows had given way under something more powerful than the storm and were being crushed upon the floor. Ellen pressed against the wall, a new kind of terror turning her helpless. She didn't move until the breaking of the glass had drifted away into silence, taking with it the bell, and the calling.

She stood still, afraid to move her eyes from the silent darkness above. What had broken upstairs? And what had broken it, she wondered. She should go up and see, she thought, but she was afraid to. Tomorrow—yes, tomorrow, she would see.

Slowly, trying to swallow her fear, Ellen backed down to the hall, her hand guiding her along the wall to her room, never for an instance taking her eyes from the open stairwell. She shut the door and for a moment listened, as if she expected something to be following her. But all she heard was the cry of the wind at her window, under the eaves.

For the rest of the night she sat up in her bed, the blanket pulled up to her chin, and stared ahead. If she told anyone what she had thought the bell said they would call her crazy. She wasn't, she hoped. But she couldn't understand. Anyway, it had ended with the breaking, and she would probably never hear it again.

But what had broken, for God's sake?

The night ended and with it, the storm. But she was exhausted, and fell asleep at daybreak. It was mid-morning before she woke and went back into the third story. The daylight gave her courage, but she climbed the stairs softly. The chill increased as she stepped from the stairs to the surrounding hall. There had to be a window out, some-where, she thought, to let in so much cold. She paused, her hand on the guard rail, and listened. But there seemed nothing out of the ordinary.

The south room, Granny had said, was her mother's—the room she had entered yesterday. She went there again, pushed open the door and left it open even though the air that met her felt like the air from the North Pole. She stood in the center of the room looking around. The windows were not broken. Neither was the mirror on the dresser. One by one, she opened every drawer in the chests and dresser. But there was not even a sliver of glass. Nor a piece of paper, for that matter.

Feeling more at ease Ellen went into her own room. There was nothing broken in there, either. She began to wonder if she had imag-ined it all. Her mind was playing tricks on her these days. There hadn't been a crashing of glass last night at all, she told herself. But she still felt that she must walk as soundlessly as possible, so that she would not be heard.

Seeking a normal activity she brought another armload of clothes from her closet and started downstairs with them. Her attention was caught suddenly by the closed door of the third bedroom. She had forgotten it. Deliberately, perhaps.

She draped the clothes over the railing and went to the closed door. She couldn't remember, in all her life, of ever being curious about that room. It had simply been there, and was always closed, as was the other, and it had not interested her. As if her mind had chosen to forget it. Was this, then, her mother's room? And what was there about her mother that made her throat tighten now? The door squeaked just slightly when she pushed it back, and the air of the room was not only frigid but was oddly and unpleasantly musty, as if something long decayed remained there. The one window was nearly covered by a long, heavy drapery that kept the light from the room.

It was a much smaller room than the others. Ellen crossed it quickly, pushed the drapery aside, and saw that the window, though veiled by long years of dust, was not broken. She turned her back to the window and looked silently about the room. Immediately the difference struck her. The bed was smaller, the furniture scratched and marred. In the corner, hanging by a long string from the high ceiling was a curious thing of odd little strips of glass.

She went closer and saw that it was an old, colorless, Oriental wind chime. She flicked it with her fingers. The sound was a faint, fine tone similar to a distant bell.

Ellen had found her bell.

She smiled, amused at herself for being afraid of a wind chime. Her smile faded as it fell silent. She didn't touch it again, but she stared at it for a long while, wondering what had made it move those other times. She blew on it, but it hung still, each sliver of glass suspended at the ends of heavy, faded red string. Only the dust stirred and moved into the air. It didn't explain the sound of breaking glass, either. But something in the back of her mind willed her to forget that, to leave it where it belonged, in the world beyond her world of reality.

Had this been her mother's room, she wondered. It seemed hardly possible. The furniture was in a deplorable state; the regular-sized bed sagged in the middle as if springs had broken. The carpet on the floor was threadbare and had holes eaten by moths or something, holes as large as a man's hand. She bent closer to examine the edges of the holes. It seemed to her that they had been cut out, chopped and ripped by something. It was a baffling thing and she decided to ask about it.

The whole room was baffling and disturbing. On looking more closely she found that the bottom of the draperies also had been chopped and shredded. She turned quickly to the drawers and began to pull them out, one by one, but there was nothing. Nothing to indicate that the room had ever held a personality—only the wind chime in the corner. And, of course, the destroyed furnishings. Ellen backed out of the room and closed the door.

She picked up her clothes and took them downstairs to her new closet. Then she went down to the ground floor. She could hear voices in Granny's favorite room, the small sitting room where the only television was, where the furniture was comfortable and fairly new and the tables strewn with magazines. It was Ellen's favorite room too. It was the room where she had cut paper dolls and played with tiny plastic toys when she was small. Her old toy box was still there, in a corner.

Tina's voice came through the partly closed door, and occasionally Granny's voice. Gentle murmurs of conversation. Ellen went on to the kitchen.

Miss Maud was at the sink getting vegetables ready to cook, and her voice rose so that Ellen could hear.

"... not such a bad storm after all it's going to turn into a regular old-fashioned Indian summer just you watch—now we'll have a month of perfect weather and I say it's time. Do you remember how many years since we've had Indian summer? I thought I'd fix a stew for supper; Tina seems to be a right nice girl and not the least haughty, I don't mind fixing a pot of stew and I've put bread to rise it'll be ready for supper ..."

"Miss Maud, do you know what happened to the east bedroom on the third floor?"

"... there's nothing like—what? East?"

"Yes. It's in a terrible state. Carpets cut and ragged and the furniture ..."

"Oh that one! No I don't know what happened. I went in to clean it a few months after I first came here to work—that was when you were four and I asked Louise and she just told me to never mind the room, just shut the door she said and never mind it so that's what I did of course I've gone in a few times to get the dust out but I never even mention that I've been in there; I thought to myself that it looked like a maniac had been turned loose in there I never saw anything like it but Miss Louise said not to mention it to her anymore so I never did and I never asked anybody else—do you reckon I ought to put onions in this stew or not? Seeings as they're just married ..."

Ellen, glad she had changed the subject, said, "Oh why not? And a hot pepper, too. We'll make them both fragrant and fiery."

"I'll bet Tina would like it with a Mexican flavor, because if the truth were known she's got a Mexican or Spanish ancestor and not too far back either ..."

"Well I like Mexican food too, and I'm not ..."

"... why she lightens her hair is a mystery to me I think if you ever bleached your pretty black hair I'd turn you over my knee and give you ..."

"If she bleaches her hair, she bleaches her eyebrows too."

"... a good whatfor—I expect she does because her eyelashes are black as ink and that's not mascara but if I were your Uncle Lance I'd try to talk her into letting herself go natural so folks could tell what she really looks like ..."

Ellen was thinking. Black hair and black eyebrows on that face that was now Tina Crayley. Suddenly she felt she could stand the house no longer. She mumbled an excuse to Miss Maud and went into the stairway room to get her coat from the closet. Then she went outside.

Snow banked in little piles against the fence glistened wetly on top, melting fast. Wind that screamed yesterday whispered today, bringing from the south a touch of warm Gulf air. The bunkhouse stretched long and low under the sun, near the long machine shed, the barns, the corrals. She went to the office first, though she saw the jeep was gone, and she went in expecting to find Rodney gone also. But he was there, leaning back in a chair, looking as if had just taken his feet off the desk or was getting ready to put them on it. His eyes squinted against the sunlight that came through the uncurtained window behind the desk, and laughed at her, and watched her. "Ah, my secretary," he said. "Just in time."

But a glance showed her his desk was nearly bare. She didn't feel like playing any teasing games the way they always had. The way a mature man plays with a worshipping too-young girl. "I want to talk to someone," she said, her eyes pleading. "Granny has—company. Miss Maud can't help me. Daddy's not here. Uncle Lance—I don't even know where he is."

The laughter had left his eyes, and only the squint remained. He put one foot on the desk after she sat down. "Your Uncle Lance," he said, "has taken the jeep and gone out on the range. Will I do?"

She looked down at her hands and pushed at the cuticle on her smooth nails. "I have some problems," she said. "I don't really understand them myself, so I don't expect anyone can solve them for me. I was halfway wishing to speak to Mr. Miller. Because he knew my mother."

# CHAPTER 3

George Miller walked slowly along the edge of the meadow, a little lonesome for the company of old Shep, wishing the old dog didn't have to ride the jeep every time it moved. No matter who drove, Rod, one of the boys, or a stranger like Lance Crayley, old Shep was ready to ride along. And because he couldn't see denying an old dog a little pleasure, George let him go. So now he walked alone on a stroll that ordinarily would have included the dog.

Still, which was out of the ordinary, his walk had a destination of sorts. He didn't know what good it would do, how it would help him to solve that thing that kept itching in his mind, but he headed for the graveyard.

At the foot of the cedar grown sandhill he paused and looked toward the house. There was no sign of life about it except a thin trail of smoke that petered out just above one of the chimneys. Something Maudie was up to, no doubt. If her eyes were as sharp as her tongue and her nose, she'd spot him for sure. He changed course, moving on around the hill as if the graveyard had never entered his mind. Then, as soon as the house was out of sight he sprinted up the hill.

By the time he reached the top his sprints had died and he was reduced to reaching for the closest cedar limb to pull himself along. He rested, puffing, saying aloud to himself, "Damn hill's getting higher every year." As he rested he started stuffing tobacco into his pipe, but let the match burn out in his fingers. If Maudie saw smoke on Crayley Hill she'd think it was smoke signals and start yelling Indian. He threw the ruined match away and put his pipe into his shirt pocket to dribble out its dry tobacco.

And then he started searching for the gravestones.

After reading several names and dates of Crayleys who had died he found the one he wanted. It was a tall, still-white stone with an angel on top. But the inscription said only *Irene Crayley. Wife of Albert. Mother of Ellen. 1927-1956.*

On the grave at the foot of the stone tufts of grass grew, their roots partly exposed by the whipping of the wind. And against the stone, piled like hay, was a collection of tumbleweeds. He booted them out, and watched them roll along over the hill. For the first time he noticed the house was visible, and he moved a few feet over, into the protection of a cedar tree. Then he stared at the grave, trying to think.

It had started the day he saw the picture that Miss Ellen claimed was her mother. There were times recently when he felt he wasn't as sharp as he used to be, but there was one thing he hadn't lost yet—his memory. And as he'd told Rod, because it kept bothering him, that picture was no more Ellen Crayley's mother than it was his own. He'd seen Irene Crayley a few times, enough to forge her permanently on his brain. As Ellen grew up he saw a second Irene Crayley. That gypsy look, black hair, black eyes, tawny skin like soft velvety leather—well, leather might not be the nicest thing to call the skin of a beautiful woman but it was the best he could do. Forget Irene Crayley's face? Never. She was one of the few women he'd ever seen that he felt he could have loved.

Sometimes he saw her walking in the yard, carrying her new baby. Twice maybe, or three times. Then, the next year, he saw her leading the toddling child. Time passed, swift in its slow seasons, and he spent the summers on the mountain range, herding, seldom coming down. When he did, when the snows started and they brought the cattle down, the grave was here, fresh. And the boss told him she had been killed in a car wreck.

He got used to not ever seeing her then, and wouldn't have thought anything about it if Miss Ellen hadn't told him the girl in the picture was her mother. There had to be a reason. The boss? Miss Louise? Why had they lied to her? He had checked the records too, and there was no death recorded. His thoughts swirled, tumbling, like the tumbleweeds moving down the hill. If Irene had not died, why had they put a stone for her? Or had she died, but not in a car? Would the boss, or Miss Louise, commit murder? The thought was new and disturbing. He had a sudden urge to dig into the grave, see what was there, and why.

He turned and walked back toward the bunkhouse, fast. He had reached the alfalfa meadow and was crossing it when he saw Ellen leave the office and go back toward the house. She didn't see him and he was glad of that. The last time they'd met he had almost spilled the beans about the death certificate. He didn't want to scare or worry her. When the time came if he had something to tell her he would, but meantime he didn't want her to wonder and fret about it.

He found Rodney standing outside the door, leaning against the wall, squinting toward the house like a man in a dream.

"Wanta talk to you, Rod."

Rodney grunted and followed him into the office, curious enough to ask, "What are you puffing so hard about, George?"

"Never mind that. Rod, what do you say about me digging into that grave?"

"*What!* Digging into a grave! What in the hell are you talking about, George?"

George decided to put a pot of coffee on and calm Rod down with a few cups. He splashed water from the cooler into the pot, on top of old grounds, and then dumped in half a cup or so of fresh coffee and flicked the hot-plate on, all the time trying to explain so that Rod wouldn't get overheated about it. "Somebody's lyin', Rod, sure as little pink rosies. Why did they tell Miss Ellen that lie about her mother? And why was there no death certificate? Rod, I want to know what's in that grave."

"For Christ's sake, George, you can't go digging up family graves."

"Rod, there's something odd about it."

"I can't think of anything any odder than you digging into that grave! What did you plan to do when you got the coffin uncovered? Lift it out by yourself? Perform an autopsy yourself?"

"I thought maybe you would help."

Rodney held his hand up, palm out toward George. "Ah no, not me. Forget it, George."

"We could get permission from the sheriff's office."

"Goddamn no! On what grounds, George? Look, let it go. Besides, Ellen was out here a while ago asking questions. She wanted to talk to you because you knew her mother. But if you do talk to her, George, you keep your mouth shut, you hear? I don't want her scared."

George stared back into Rodney's hot eyes, and then he asked the most logical question he could think of. "How can I keep my mouth shut and talk at the same time?"

Rodney smiled and sank down into his chair. He raised his long legs and carefully placed both feet on the desk. "You know what I mean."

George asked, "What was it she wanted to know?"

"She didn't know what she wanted. She'd gone into this room, on the top floor of the house, where she thinks her mother lived, and found the place more or less chopped up. Nobody tells her anything. I think she's wondering if her mother was all right in the head." He fixed George with the intense gaze he used when he wanted all truth and no fooling or horsing around. "Was she, George?"

"Why sure she was!" George felt it almost a personal insult. He was ready to fight for his honor. "She was a beautiful woman, I told you that."

"I know, I know. But how many times did you talk to her?"

"Talk?" George settled back. "I never did talk to her."

"That's what I figured. All you know is how she looked, right?"

"Well, I reckon so. But ..."

"You tell Ellen that when she asks you. Just tell her her mom was beautiful. And I don't see any reason to tell her the picture is not Irene Crayley. Whatever reason the folks had, it must have been a good one. Now, I've got to get out of here and get some work done."

"What about the coffee?"

"Let it steep awhile. It ought to be about right when I get back."

Rodney went out, a tall man with a straight back and strong, square shoulders, and dark hair that was curly enough to look all the time like a woman's fingers had just gone through it, and long enough to make him look like he needed a haircut. George kept his own hair short. If it touched his ears, he felt like a shaggy sheep dog. He'd never get used to the modern cuts, or un-cuts, but he couldn't help wishing he could walk out in Rodney's shoes, young again, alive and healthy, able to climb a hill without puffing.

He turned the coffee off, collected the dirty cups and went through the door into the adjoining room. It was a long room with bunkbeds along one wall, and a coal-eating pot-belly at one end surrounded by chairs. The place of honor was taken by a portable TV that was as dusty as an old pair of boots. George saw the dust but went on by as usual, and through another door into the kitchen. A big beef roast in the oven was sending out beacon signals. George dumped a pan of potatoes into the sink, swished a little water on them, and then tossed them into the oven to bake. They scattered and rolled in the bottom like walnuts falling from a tree, and the water sizzled and spat. From the cabinet he got six plastic plates and tossed them onto the big table that stood at one end of the room. Then he tossed after them six forks and a handful of knives and spoons. That done, he sat down to think.

He couldn't imagine the Crayley family, Albert or his mother, committing a murder. But stranger things had happened, he knew. They'd been good to him. Treated him like an equal, not a hired hand. Let him stay on when he retired and kept right on paying him wages for the little things he did. Rod was right, he couldn't raise a fuss, call the sheriff or anything. But for his own peace of mind, he'd sure like to know what was in that grave.

The sound of the jeep reached his ears just a moment before it stopped outside the kitchen door. He got up and went out. Old Shep had a smile on his long, part collie muzzle that equaled nothing. He hopped out and came to greet George. Lance Crayley came walking around. He was dressed up like a western dude, George thought, as if he'd never lived on a real ranch. But then he hadn't, much. He had gone away to school when he was twelve or thirteen, George couldn't remember exactly, a military school or something, and hadn't been home much since.

"Beats riding a horse," Lance said, smiling.

George nodded, though he really didn't agree. For himself he'd still take a horse. "Easier on the horses I reckon," he said. He patted old Shep. "Have a good time, old feller?"

Lance answered, "He sure did. He'd ride all the time, wouldn't he?" In a suddenly softer voice Lance was saying, "Here comes my childbride. Have you met her, George? Come along and meet her."

George followed reluctantly. He'd caught a couple of glimpses of the new wife when he took care of the house fires, enough to see that she was what the boys in the bunkhouse called "stacked." She came running now, laughing, her blonde hair bouncing on top of her head, her arms out, reminding George of a certain commercial on TV. Lance grabbed her up and gave her a big kiss, then turned her toward George. For the first time, George saw her full-face. He saw her black eyes and figured immediately that her hair was bleached. "Howdy,

Ma'am," he said, reaching up to tip his hat and fumbling with air, no hat to tip. Meeting people made him nervous, always had. He'd forgotten he wasn't wearing a hat.

Suddenly her smile was gone and she was staring at him. He returned her stare because her face, sober, mouth small, eyes deep-set and dark as two hunks of coal, looked familiar. He never forgot a face, yet he couldn't place her. His brain was struggling again, muddy, flooding river, as he tried to remember where he had seen her.

"Hello," she said, "nice to know you." And quickly turned her back. With her arm around Lance's waist she began pulling him along toward the house.

George stood still, watching her go, trying to bring back that face and put it where it belonged in his memory. Face shaped like a diamond. Something about it that looked mean as hell, no matter now nice she was trying to pretend to be. A face that changed in laughter like a sky clearing. And likewise, a face that changed to the dark threat of a coming storm. She looked back once, a long, piercing, hostile look that turned George uncomfortably away. He went back into the kitchen. Old Shep came along and lay down on the wornout pants in the corner. George had put them there when Shep was a pup and they hadn't been moved many times since. But old Shep was comfortable that way, and so was George. A little dirt didn't bother either one of them.

But not remembering a face did, and George swore to himself that he'd place her or die trying. Out loud, to old Shep, he said, "There aren't many choices. Let's see. Outside of being here on the ranch since I was nineteen I lived on my uncle's ranch. Growed up there. Been to Cheyenne a couple of times. Denver once. And—oh yeah. Went to the carnival every year there for a while. But she's not that old." He sat down. "Be damned." Old Shep thumped his tail on the floor in sympathy, and George kept thinking. After awhile, when he heard voices outside and knew the boys were coming in for supper, he decided to sleep on it a few times.

"My memory is failing me after all, Shep. I'll have to let it steep awhile. "

After supper a couple of the Boys went off on dates, one washed dishes; Rod too dressed up and went to town, saying nothing about his plans for the evening— and George went to the shed where the coal was kept, loaded a couple of buckets and took them to the house. He heard her before he saw her. As always.

"... freeze to death around here waiting for you I had to get out and get my own coal this morning and ..."

He saw she was up to her elbows in sudsy, steaming dish water. "Warm day today," he said. "It'd take a frog to freeze on a day like this."

"... and that's the unhandiest place I ever saw, it looks to me maybe a man could do a little better job of fixing it so's a woman could handle it if he's not going to do."

George went on, into the long central hall. No one was in the dining room. He dumped a few lumps of coal into the fire, and then climbed the back stairs. One bucket he put down outside Miss Ellen's door. The other he took to Miss Louise's room. Everyone evidently was downstairs. He went out again and returned with two more buckets—one he left in the hall upstairs for Lance, and the other he took down to the sitting room.

They were there, Lance smoking, carrying on a soft-voiced conversation with his mother. Miss Ellen just sitting, looking at a magazine. And over by the window, looking out, the one he wanted to see. She turned when he entered and looked at him, straight, cold, unfriendly. Then without speaking she turned her back and went to a knick-knack cabinet and pretended to be busy. George took time in building up the fire, poking at it, doing things that didn't need doing, trying to get a good look at Lance's wife without letting on what he was up to. But she kept her back turned, and he knew that she was aware that he could recognize her. And if that was the case, then she knew him.

And she didn't want him to remember her.

He left the room, finally, with his memory still in the dark.

Maud was rinsing the sink when he entered the kitchen. "Pretty slow getting around tonight aren't you? When a fire's built it's built and …"

"Did you ever see that woman before, Maud?"

She stopped, her head half-turned toward him. "*What* woman."

"Lance's wife."

"Tina, no I never saw her before—why?"

"I have."

Maud turned completely, surprise taking her voice for a moment. Then, "Well? What do you mean by that? Who is she? Where'd you see her? You mean she's not what she claims to be?"

"I never said that. I just said I've seen her before. But I can't for the life of me place her."

Maud snorted and turned back to the sink. "She probably looks like someone you saw on television because it's not likely you ever saw her before you watch too much television …"

George went out shaking his head. No use trying to talk to Maud.

Dark had come while he was building fires, with a rise in the wind. It swept cool and fresh against his face. In the east a large, glowing ball climbed, throwing shadows on the west of things. Full moon tonight. George stopped and looked for awhile, not thinking of anything except the beauty in a full moon. He watched until it peeled free from the horizon like something being born, then he turned his back to it and walked on to the bunkhouse, following his own long shadow.

He was sitting by the dying fire, smoking a dying pipe, when Rodney came in. The other boys had already come in and gone to bed, and George was waiting for Rodney. Though it was past midnight, a late hour for George, he had a question to ask. "Rod, ever see Lance's wife?"

"Yeah."

"You remember that time in Cheyenne we all got drunk and went to that cathouse? She wasn't one of them girls, was she?"

Rodney made a startled sound in his throat that was a half-hearted attempt at a laugh and a cuss word rolled into one. His fingers paused in unbuttoning his shirt. "George, what's the matter with you, you crazy or something? You better not let anybody else hear you say that, not if you want to stay on here."

George kept his voice low and insistent. "*Was she*, Rod?"

"Hell no! What do you think! What ever gave you that idea?"

"I've seen her somewhere, and I can't remember. After all these years of bragging how I never forgot a face, you expect me to give up on it?"

"Maybe you're wrong for once. Maybe she just reminds you of somebody. Why don't you go to bed?" He went into the bathroom and George stayed with his cold stove and his cold pipe, chewing and staring. He wasn't going to bed though. He had a plan. George sat, unmoving, until Rodney began the soft rhythmic snore that proved sufficiently that he was asleep; then, stealthily, George tucked his pipe into his shirt pocket and went out the front door so that old Shep wouldn't hear him and try to follow. He didn't want anyone along tonight, not even the dog.

The full moon spread a clear light over the landscape. The huge old house was a combination of silvered roof, reflecting windows, and black walls. Deep shadows lay just to the east of it now that the moon was reaching toward the western mountains. George chose his steps carefully to avoid noise, and went into the dark interior of the machine shed. In a minute he was out again carrying a pick and a shovel. His eyes turned again toward the house, and for the brief flash of a half thought, a shadow within the shadows moved, blending into nothing.

George stopped, squinting. Had he seen something that didn't want to be seen? Confusion seemed to be taking him lately. His mind must be going bad, as well as his eyes. To make sure, because he didn't believe his own perceptions, he moved slowly toward the house. In the edge of the shadows he stopped. There where he had thought something moved was the end of a long hedge of untrimmed lilacs. A bird probably flew into them, he decided, and turned his back to the house, walking toward the graveyard on Crayley Hill. The back of his neck tingled every step of the way, and several times he turned and looked back. But no one was watching him after all. Only the house with its silver roof. Cottonwood trees hid the barns and the bunkhouse. He wished he had gone the other way around so that the house had been hidden instead. Finally he reached the hill and the cover of cedar trees, and he decided his conscience had been pricking at the back of his neck. But if he would let a little thing like that stop him his name wasn't George Miller.

Her grave was in the moonlight, and he paused long enough to say softly, "Forgive me if I'm disturbing a grave that oughtn't to be disturbed. But if I thought that was it, I wouldn't be here." He began to dig.

If he found an honest to goodness coffin he didn't know what he would do. Just cover it up and pretend he'd never dug there. Because if the woman had been murdered, she would have been buried without a proper coffin, he figured. In fact, if she had been murdered it was his idea she wouldn't be buried there at all. And that was what he was expecting to find—an empty grave. Or that is, no grave at all. Just a headstone. He dug hard and fast, a full seven feet in length and down, down, four, five. Nothing. His heart pounded in his chest, and he threw the pick to the top of the ground and dug in with the shovel and threw out the soil, building a small mountain on the west of the hole that was no grave after all.

He paused to rest, to lay his shovel aside and reach for the pick to loosen the deeper soil, his hand touching dirt clods. Surprised, he raised himself up over the edge of the hole and looked around for the pick. It was gone. He was ready to cuss himself out for shoveling dirt onto it when something behind him moved.

He whirled, looking up. The first thing he saw was the pick, upright, in a hand that shown pale in the moonlight, and then his eyes found in horror the diamond-shaped face of the girl who stood there. She was drawing her lips back in silent laughter as both hands raised the pick slowly over her head. George stared up at her, unable to move except to reach his hands helplessly out against what she was going to do to him, because now he recognized her too late.

His hoarse voice screamed once, "Ellen!" Before the pointed iron of the pickhead killed him.

<h1 style="text-align:center">CHAPTER 4</h1>

Ellen woke suddenly, and lay tense and still, listening. There had been a sound, she wasn't sure what; now there was nothing but a soft whisper of wind at the window. She had opened the draperies before she went to bed, and a long, slender, diaphanous body of moonlight folded over the sill, the floor, the foot of her bed. Her door was still shut, and for some reason that surprised her. For the first time in her life she wished for a lock on her door.

Quietly she put back her blanket and slid her feet to the floor. She started to open the door and paused, her fingers sliding away from the knob. The hall would be long and dark with only the dim light at the stairway. She had never felt so afraid to go into the hall before.

After a moment of listening at the door she went softly to the window and looked out. The cottonwood trees cast shadows like black lace trembling in the wind, the bunkhouse was dark and silent. Her eyes moved to the rounded rise of Crayley Hill, and among the scattered black cedars she saw the faint glow of something that must be a tombstone. She would have liked to have gone there now, this night, as she did a week ago, but the thought of walking through the hall stopped her. If only there was a door on the steep and narrow stairway that rose at the end, a door she could close and lock.

She turned away from the window and went back to bed. Tonight there was no sound other than the wind, but still she was restless and nervous. She tried to go back to sleep but succeeded only in dozing and waking. At one point she thought she heard footsteps outside her door. She sat up in bed and listened intently for several minutes, but like the first soundless sound that had awakened her, it no longer existed.

Ellen was on time for breakfast. Tina and Lance were already there, Tina looking as if she never required any sleep at all, and Lance with purple bags under each eye and a sag of weakness in his jowls as if he had been drugged and was fighting a hangover.

Tina giggled and said, "If you two aren't a pair! Why do you get up so early if you need so much more sleep?"

Ellen started to reply that she hadn't been able to sleep anyway, but at that moment Miss Maud came pushing through the swinging door with a tray of sausages, pancakes, coffee pot, a pitcher of orange juice, and many opinions.

"... all you're going to get because the fire's out now that George is never around when he's supposed to be and I'm taking Louise's breakfast up to her room so if George comes in while I'm upstairs tell him to bring the usual amount even though the temperature is going towards eighty today according to the weatherman now what'd I tell you about Indian summer? Not even spring-time is like Indian ..."

She went out again, her voice trailing away into the back stairs. Tina made a face of annoyance.

"That Maudie, doesn't she ever do anything but talk? I don't think the woman even breathes."

"Well," said Ellen, laughing lightly. "I've wondered, myself. But she does work."

"I think I could find someone better than that. Younger, more capable, and quieter."

"Miss Maud has been here since I can remember."

Heavy steps, the sound of a door closing somewhere in the kitchen, ended the conversation. George, Ellen thought, and lifted the small glass of orange juice to her lips. When the door opened and the dark and handsome face of Rodney looked in she nearly dropped the whole glass. Tina's eyes flashed from the door to Ellen to the glass in the suddenly unsteady hand, and took on an amused smirk. Now she knows, Ellen thought, and wondered why she felt it such a disaster that Tina know she was in love with Rodney.

"Good morning," Rodney said, smiling at each in turn. "Can I come in?"

Lance grunted and made an effort to rise a bit out of his slump and Ellen got to her feet and went to the breakfront for another cup.

"Please do," she said. "Drink a cup of good coffee for a change."

His smile was especially for her, warm and hypnotic, drawing her to him. At least she felt it that way.

"Do you think I'd survive it?" he asked. "I've been drinking George's coffee for so many years my guts are corroded." As if he had suddenly become aware of more elegant surroundings and people, he looked at Tina and said, "If you'll excuse my language. The kid is used to me, and I forgot where I was for a minute."

So he was still calling her the kid. Couldn't he see she had grown up for gosh sakes?

Lance grunted again, and Tina smiled, a tight little smile that left her eyes cold and waiting like, Ellen thought, the shining bellies of two black widow spiders. She hastily turned her back to Tina and poured the coffee for Rodney.

Tina's voice, as smooth as a spider's silk web, filled the pause. "You're the ranch foreman, aren't you?"

"Yes Ma'am."

Lance grunted, "Manager, Childbride, manager."

"What's the difference?" Tina asked.

"Not much," Rodney said.

And Lance added, "About ten thousand a year."

"How interesting," Tina murmured. "Really, all you do is tell the other men what to do, isn't it?"

"Something like that," Rodney said. "Which brings me to my mission. One of my men is missing this morning." He looked up at Ellen. "Has George been around?"

"Why, no. Not at all in fact. Miss Maud was saying something about it. I don't remember ..."

Tina broke in with, "Who could ever remember what she says, she says so much. Is George the old man?"

Rodney answered. "Uh—yeah. I guess you could call him that. Though I wouldn't advise it."

"But he is an old man whether he admits it or not. He might have decided to leave," Tina said. "Old men do strange things sometimes."

"Without his clothes? Or his dog?" Rodney asked.

Tina seemed surprised. "He had a dog?"

"Yeah. Well, I guess the dog has him—and the rest of us as well. He spent as much time out with the boys as with George. Depending on who was doing the most interesting thing at the time. He was still asleep in his corner when I got up."

Ellen said, "Do you mean George wasn't there when you got up? He usually cooks breakfast, doesn't he?"

"Yeah, he does. This is the first time anything like this ever happened. The stoves were cold, his bed was already made. Or never slept in. When I last saw him, last night, he was by the stove smoking his pipe ..." He stopped abruptly, looked down into his coffee, and then he looked up straight into Tina's eyes.

Ellen saw the look, saw the smile Tina gave him, and the answering half-smile from Rodney, and tight fingers of fear knotted in her throat. It was a look of physical attraction, she felt, and was sick with the thought. She wanted to tear Rodney's eyes away from Tina, remind him she was married. But what difference did marriage make anymore?

"Did you see George this morning, Uncle Lance?" Ellen asked. "Did he bring fuel to your room—to you and Tina?" That was too obvious, she thought, and felt her face flush with embarrassment. She saw Rodney's amused smile, his eyes on her profile, but she tried to ignore it.

"Naw," said Lance, "The room was cold. Childbride ran naked to the bathroom."

Tina said, "Stop calling me that. Go wash your face, and then go to town and get somebody to come out here and put a heating system in this old tomb." The emotion under her words seemed to Ellen to be filled with anger.

"I guess I'll have to," Lance said. "Whether Mother likes it or not."

Rodney said to Ellen, "What I'm afraid of is he's gone for a walk or something and had a heart attack. I sent the boys on to work, figuring to give George time to come home on his own, in case he just decided to walk out, but I'd like to look around just the same. I was wondering if you'd look with me."

"Yes, of course. I'll get my jacket. It's in the closet on the way out."

Rodney said goodbye to Tina and Lance and they went out into warm sunshine and a rather gentle southern wind. Ellen turned to face it, to let it push her hair back. Rodney's hand touched her hair unexpectedly, smoothing it behind her ear, and she had to gather all her self-control to keep from groaning with delight.

"What happened to the braids?" he asked softly, standing almost against her, looking down into her face. "Suddenly you don't have braids anymore". The other hand touched the other side of her head, smoothing her hair back, pulling her closer so that for a moment her body was pressed to his. He pulled her head back and bent over her and kissed her lightly on the tip of the nose, then he pushed her away.

She would have liked to have said something carefree and teasing, but she could hardly get her breath. One of his big hands closed around her hand and they began to walk. She wondered what he would have done if she had thrown her arms around his neck and kissed him on the mouth. Pulled her right down there and taken her, probably, and then walked off and left forever. Well, anyway, it was a thought.

A man as handsome as Rodney, though, would have women turning the aggressor all the time, and that kind of man had to be caught by letting him do the catching. Women's lib or no. Instinct warned her of that. Just so Tina didn't draw him away now. Ellen kept her hand relaxed in his, her fingers only lightly touching. They paused on the walk and Rodney's eyes searched the landscape, from the river and cottonwood trees south, to the ranch buildings, to Crayley's Hill north.

"Have you got any ideas?" she asked. "Where did he go when he walked?"

"I never saw him anywhere except around the place, and especially his vegetable garden. I think he vented all his frustrations, and feelings, on his garden. He gets a lot of pleasure out of that garden. And," he grinned quickly at her, "so do I. We all hate to see frost. He's still bringing vegetables in though. Well, let's take a walk in that direction. There was a full moon last night; who knows, he might have decided to dig parsnips."

The garden spot looked wilted and soggy with small patches of snow in the shade. Rodney shoved the toe of his boot into the softness of rotting cabbage leaves.

"Not even a footprint," he said. "He hasn't been in the garden since the snow."

Ellen looked at the closed bunkhouse. "Where's old Shep?"

"He went out with the boys. As I said, he is everybody's dog. Still, he's nobody's fool. He missed George too, and was sniffing and whining around George's bunk. I thought maybe he might be able to trail George, but old Shep's a traveling dog mostly, a Jeep rider. He didn't even know what I was trying to get him to do. So I sent him on his way with the boys. No point in him hanging around George's bunk whining. Might as well be happy." His hand tightened on hers until her fingers hurt, then relaxed and held her gently again. "Do you think you're up to a walk down the road to the river?"

"Sure."

They walked along the sandy road, the soles of their shoes collecting the small, sharp, goathead thorns that seemed to appear like sand-like pebbles on a beach, from no obvious source. Rodney constantly scanned the fields both right and left, and Ellen knew he was honestly worried. When they reached the river they stood on the low bank and looked down into water that was spread so thinly between its wide and sandy banks that it was hardly a foot deep anywhere. She wished she could brush away the look of worry in Rodney's eyes.

"Rodney, maybe he just decided to take a vacation. Maybe he went up to a cabin in the foothills. Or to town."

"Yes, maybe so," he said absently, looking north toward the house and Crayley Hill. From there the peaked rooflines and carved gables, porches sticking out like bird perches, made of the house something from an inhospitable past.

"Let's get back," he said. "I'll drive up to the cabin. He spent most of his time there in the early years. I have to go up there anyway and may have to stay a day or two, depending on how well Jack and Pierce are doing."

Ellen knew he was straw-grasping now. She hadn't been worried before; she didn't know Mr. Miller's habits as well as Rodney did, but the general feeling of tragedy began to grow. By the time they had reached the shed, and she watched Rodney drive away toward the mountains, she felt as sure as Rodney that something had happened to George Miller.

She didn't want to go back to the house, and decided to look again into all the buildings Rodney had said he'd searched. The bunkhouse was still and cold, the only stove used for breakfast evidently the hotplate borrowed from the office. She stood in the middle of the long room and looked around, wondering if some of Mr. Miller's clothes might be missing. But she didn't know anything about his clothes. After awhile she went out and looked through the tool and machine sheds, and even climbed into the loft of the hay barn. And finally the coal shed. After that she didn't know where to look.

Up by the house a van that had Acme Heating printed in yellow letters on the door had parked, and two men, with Uncle Lance, were looking at the foundation of the house. She watched them for a moment, until suddenly her attention was drawn to a window on the third story. A face was outlined against the glass, a white diamond that seemed disembodied, a ghost in the shadowed room, and for one unreasoning instant terror shook Ellen. But then she saw it was Tina, looking out. Looking at her? Ellen turned, as if she hadn't seen the face, and began to walk, going into the protection of the cottonwoods and around the edge of the alfalfa meadow toward Crayley Hill.

It was her old room where Tina looked through the window. Why? Still exploring? Yes, probably. She seemed to have a lot of interest in the house.

Ellen stopped by her mother's gravestone and looked again at the house. She wished she could talk to somebody about her feelings, and softly aloud she said, "But Granny likes her. Am I just being childish and selfish because I wish they would leave?" Her fingers touched the letters carved in the stone, and like one reading braille she traced the words: *Irene Crayley. Wife of Albert. Mother of Ellen. 1927-1956.* She glanced down and saw that tumbleweeds had pushed up against the stone. She brushed them aside and sent them on their way. And then she turned to leave.

She stopped, looking back at the grave. There was a difference in it, and for a moment she couldn't decide what it was. The sand stirred in the wind, moving between the bulge of the grave and the headstone.

The bulge.

The body of the grave was more rounded than usual, as if it were slowly rising.

She stared, frowning, for the first time in her life afraid here too, a peculiar sensation of horror stirring in her mind. She backed away, still staring at the slight roundness. Had it been that way before and she hadn't noticed, she wondered. It didn't even matter. She knew she would never be able to come to her mother's grave again. She turned then and walked quickly away.

Avoiding the kitchen and Miss Maud, Ellen went up the back stairs to her room. She was still thinking of the grave, the roundness she had never noticed before, and her room seemed now the sanctuary the hill once had been. She stretched out on her bed, more tired than she had realized, and laid her head on her arms.

The house was quiet. The whole world seemed quiet. The whine of the wind was soft and soothing, and encouraged her to sleep, playing its own unique lullaby. Footsteps above her brought her fully alert though, and she sat up. Tina was still upstairs? The steps were leisurely, pausing now and then. Still, Ellen listened. Then suddenly the steps were rapid, running, disappearing for a moment, then coming down the stairs, striking the wooden steps, pounding, in a frantic way. Or perhaps angry. Ellen slid off the bed and went to the door in time to see Tina come out of the stairwell.

She stopped and stared at Ellen. "Oh. Here you are. What do you want?"

The question, and the way it was spoken, stunned Ellen for a moment. But then she said, "I don't want anything."

A deep frown made Tina's small face look childishly peevish. "Then what did you call me for?"

"I didn't call you."

"But I heard you!"

"I didn't call you," Ellen repeated, carefully emphasizing each word and trying to hold her temper. She didn't like being accused of anything in that tone.

"Then who did?" Tina cried. "Someone called!"

"Not that I heard," Ellen said.

Tina stopped frowning at Ellen and her gaze wandered the hallway thoughtfully. "Perhaps it was Lance," she said abruptly, walking away. "He's outside."

Ellen watched her walk down the hall, then she went back into her room to rest. She thought of Tina upstairs, in her old room, probably going through the desk, seeing personal things she hadn't yet moved, and was unable to rest. Even her old diary was upstairs. She had started it when she was fifteen, and all the love notes she would have liked to give to Rodney were in the book. She didn't want anyone reading that, especially Tina. She had a feeling Tina would take a malicious delight in it.

She hurried up the stairs and into her room. It was the largest of the three, a virtual cavern of a place with corners tucked in beside the built-out closets, and a high ceiling. She hadn't really noticed before how large it was. She went immediately to the desk. The diary was still there, in plain sight, beside a box of stationery. Tina evidently hadn't seen it. Perhaps, after all, she was misjudging Tina. Her strange dislike of Uncle Lance's childbride probably had no basis at all, except her own imagination.

She slipped the diary into the pocket of her tunic, and then she emptied the drawers of the desk onto the bed, making a rather large pile of the odds and ends that had been collected. She stood back and surveyed it, wondering what to do with it as there was no desk in her new room, and getting the old monster downstairs would be too much trouble. Anyway, she'd have to get a laundry basket to carry her collection down. If any of it had been touched it didn't show, and she wondered what Tina had been doing in her room for so long. Whatever she had wanted in the room, it hadn't involved the desk. Of course the only thing that Ellen cared about was the diary. She had a notion to dump the pile on the bed into the wastebasket.

The sound reached her consciousness in so fine a tone that it seemed to have been swirling in her brain long before she was aware of it. All warmth left her body as she listened, standing still, daring hardly to move her hands away from the old letters she had reached for, afraid they would be heard and draw that other substance toward her. She knew what it was now. It wasn't a bell at all. It was the glass chime in the closed, small, tortured bedroom. But what was making it move? Now she knew what Tina had heard. Like a tiny, far-away voice it was calling *Tin-a—Tin-a*. The door of that room must be open, she thought desperately, reaching for logic. It was open and bringing a draft up the open stairs. Tina had probably left it open. Ellen tiptoed to the doorway, her eyes searching the wall across the way, reluctant yet determined. But the door was not open. Then, she thought, it had to be the window. Tina had gone in, opened the window, heard the chime, and thought someone was calling her.

Ellen slowly crossed the hallway, went around the railing and to the door. The sound was much clearer now. She gathered courage by telling herself she was acting a fool, and opened the door.

The room was shadowed and darkened, the drapery hanging limp and still on a closed window. She stepped into the room just far enough to see the wind chime in the corner. It swayed gently, as if pushed by a breath of wind in a room that was stuffy and so airless Ellen felt suffocated. As she watched, one slender rectangle of glass touched another, but the sound seemed more to be coming from somewhere high up in the shadowed ceiling, a frail, mournful, little cry—Teen-a, Tin-a. Ellen stepped backwards out of the room and closed the door as softly as she could. Then, like Tina before her, she ran down the stairs.

In her room she listened again, but the chime was silent now. She took the diary from her pocket and slipped it under her pillow. Her thoughts, though, remained with the chime. Something moved it in a room that seemed to have little air. She shuddered and tried to put the thought away from her. She wondered if Rodney had found George, and felt that he hadn't, and never would.

EVERYTHING SEEMED DIFFERENT. That pleasant feeling that had always surrounded the ranch was missing. Since Tina came. No. Before that. Since she had come home from Denver. It was a feeling in the atmosphere of the house. As if something had come home with her. Or had been waiting when she arrived. Tina couldn't be blamed for that. The chime, that was the difference. That first night when she had heard the sound and thought it was a bell somewhere; since then everything had seemed different, as if something in the house, and even in the air outside the house, was growing, gaining strength, taking control. Making the chime move.

Ellen left her room and started toward the back stairs, but a glance at the other stairway, so close, rising into the third floor, stopped her. She turned toward the more distant front stairs, and ran.

In the downstairs hall she slowed and was able to walk with some dignity into the kitchen.

"... sure picked a peculiar time to run off if you ask me ..." Miss Maud, at the sink, ripped open a head of lettuce. "... going to have a cold lunch because my back's too weak today to be carrying heavy coal buckets around like ..."

"I'll bring some coal in for you," Ellen offered, glad to hear the comfortable, familiar complaints from Miss Maud.

"No you won't, you better not let me catch you carrying coal that's his job that George what business he had sneaking ..."

"Well, not really, Miss Maud. He just voluntarily took it on himself to do so."

"... off no telling where it's a good thing Lance is getting a heating system put in is all I've got to say."

Ellen laughed, unable to resist the opportunity to tease Miss Maud a little. "You're kidding."

Miss Maud ignored her. "All I've got to say as I was saying, it takes a man in love to change things you just watch—let her ask and he'll start walking on his hands ..."

"Miss Maud, what would make that wind chime in the old bedroom move when there's nothing to move it?"

"... she wants a heating system we'll have a heating—what?"

Ellen sat on the kitchen stool at the cabinet and reached for a lettuce leaf. Without looking at the lettuce, Miss Maud tore off a leaf and handed it to her. "That wind chime," Ellen said. "It moves. Why?"

Miss Maud's hands were still, folded in front of her. Water dripped from her fingers. "*What* wind chime?" She always sounded so surprised when she asked a question.

"Upstairs. In that room."

"The room that's been messed up?"

"Yes." Amazed, Ellen looked up at Miss Maud. She had never held Miss Maud's attention so long before that she could remember.

"You say it moves?"

"Yes."

"That's impossible—how can it?" She abruptly wiped her hands on her apron and started toward the door to the stairway. "I never saw any chime there that I can remember of course I haven't been in that room for over a year now not since the last time I dusted it and I always did as little as I could and got out ..."

Ellen followed behind her up the two flights of stairs, comfortable in the flood of her words, her matter-of-fact advance on the unknown. Miss Maud didn't hesitate to open the door. Still advancing like an army she went to the corner to look at the chime. She gave it a determined glare, her nose scarcely two inches away. It hung as still and limp as the draperies.

"... funny I never saw it before I guess I just didn't take the time to look up but it's not moving now in fact it's covered in dust and don't look like it moved since it was hung there; it must have took a ladder plus a tall man to get it hung to the ceiling—but you say you saw it moving? It must have been a draft of some kind whatever it was it wasn't much because it doesn't take much to make wind chimes move they're made a purpose that way ..."

Her head tipped back, her gaze following the supporting string to the ceiling. "... wonder who on earth it belonged to? "

"I don't know."

Ellen stood in the doorway looking at the chime as Miss Maud flipped it lightly with a finger. The sound was a series of tinkles that floated away as the chime stopped moving. Miss Maud turned, her gaze taking in the room. "This place looks like somebody's been at it with a hammer and a chisel and I'm surprised the chime is still there and that Tina did—you know she's been looking the place over so maybe she moved the chime— anyways lunch never fixed itself and I'm not getting it fixed either so if you want me to cut the chime down I will. It looks to me like something that needs to be thrown in the trash ..."

"No," Ellen said, and then wondered why. Maybe because it might have belonged to her mother. Or maybe because the chime seemed to have acquired a life of its own, no matter how weird that life might be. She closed the door firmly behind them as Miss Maud started back to the kitchen, with a silent, half-promise that she would not open it again.

Ellen watched for Rodney, but he did not return. She went early to her room after dinner and sat looking out toward the bunkhouse, watching for the lights of the ranch pickup. After an hour that seemed endless she decided Rodney had stayed at the cabin and watching for him, hoping he had found George, would be futile. She closed her draperies and went to bed.

· · ·

HER SLEEP WAS RESTLESS. She woke and slept again. The chime tinkled faintly, calling, through her dreams, or ...

Her room, though darkened when she went to bed, was softly lighted, and she raised herself to see at the foot of her bed the diamond-shaped face, only this time it was different. The black hair had been changed to white hair that floated above the face, and she stood unmoving, looking at her, just looking and looking.

The scream burst in her ears, then she was crushing it back with both hands, staring at the face, hearing footsteps running in the hall. A light flashed on, and she saw it was Lance at the door, and by her bed, Tina, looking frightened, turning toward the doorway where Lance stood blinking, his hand still on the switch.

Tina too was half-screaming, half-sobbing, her hands clutching and clawing at Lance's arm. "What's the matter with her?" she cried. "What's the matter with her? Lance, I only came to see what she wanted. She keeps calling me. I only came to see what she wanted! "

He held her to his chest and glared over her head at Ellen. More steps, and Miss Maud was peeking over Lance's shoulder, her thin lips pressed hard together, her eyes round and wondering. Ellen, shaking so hard she could hardly get her arms into her robe, slid out of bed and stood looking at them. She tried to explain. "I—I was asleep. I didn't know it was Tina. I was s-startled, that's all. I'm sorry I scared her."

"You okay now?" Lance asked her.

Ellen nodded.

"Then we'll go back to bed. Come on, childbride." They disappeared from sight, his arms holding her close.

At last Miss Maud opened her lips. "What you need is warm milk and I'll go get it and be right back ..."

An unsteady voice down the hall called, "Ellen? Was that you?"

"Your granny ..." Miss Maud said, "... bound to be worried so you go see about her and I'll bring both of you a glass of milk to her room."

Ellen nodded, though she hated warm milk. When she was

younger she had poured it in potted plants. She went down to Granny's room. The old lady was sitting up in bed nearly lost among pillows and thick, old-fashioned comforters. She wore a ruffled nightcap that made her look like something out of Dickens.

"Did I hear you crying out again?" her granny asked.

Ellen climbed up onto the bed and laid her head on the pillow beside Granny, where the old lady's small hand could caress her forehead.

"Yes. I'm a baby. A silly, squealing, imaginative female."

"Nonsense. Don't run yourself down. There's nothing wrong with being an imaginative female. Was it the same old nightmare?"

"I thought it was," Ellen said. "But it turned out that it wasn't a dream at all. Tina had come in. She woke me and scared me silly. I guess I upset the whole house. Sorry."

Granny patted her. "Don't worry about it. We'll explain tomorrow to Lance and Tina about those old nightmares you have sometimes and they'll understand."

Ellen lay silent for a moment, soothed by the hand. "Granny— I'm scared deep down. It's getting worse."

"Why, what do you mean, Ellen?"

"Well, like the chime upstairs in that bedroom. And who ruined the furniture in that room, Granny? Whose chime was it? Not my mother's—surely not hers."

The hand on the forehead was still, and there was no answer. Ellen raised her head and saw that her grandmother was staring beyond her, drawn back to other years.

"Granny?"

Her grandmother blinked and looked at her. "The room? Well we had a young guest once who was a bit destructive. I should have had the bedroom cleaned out, but I just never got around to it. Furniture is so hard to get up and down those old stairs. Let's just leave the door closed and don't think about it."

Ellen had never before felt that her grandmother was lying to her, but now she did. To accuse her of it would be unthinkable. She would have to find out some other way.

Her grandmother was asking, "Has that been disturbing you? Is that all?" She tried to make it sound unimportant, Ellen knew, but it sounded forced instead.

"No," Ellen said. "There's another thing, Granny. Sometimes I think I must be going out of my mind. But you know the girl in my nightmares?"

Her grandmother nodded.

"It's Tina, Granny. And yet, how can it be?"

The old lady stared into her eyes, asking, "What are you saying?" The pink left her cheeks and her throat, and her forehead looked damp suddenly.

Alarmed, Ellen sat up and reached for her hand. "Granny? Are you feeling all right?"

"Yes," the old lady said impatiently, "just tell me what you meant."

"Tina? The girl in my nightmares. They're the same, Granny. I mean they look the same. How can it be when I've never seen her before? One is a child, the other a woman; one has black hair, the other ..." But all color had left Louise Crayley's face, and her hands fluttered to her chest. Ellen, frantic, began to search through the drawer in the bed table for the bottle of pills that Granny took for her spells. The wrinkled little hand reached out toward her.

"No—no ..." Gaining breath, and with breath, strength. "I'm all right. I'm all right. Just relax and sit here awhile. Did I hear Maud say something about milk?"

# CHAPTER 5

L ouise lay in her bed, in the dark of her room, and stared wide-eyed, thinking. The house was quiet again, Maud gone with partly empty glasses, grumbling because a few drops of that awful milk remained in the bottoms. Ellen had gone back to her room. She wondered now if Ellen was safe there. If she would be safe anywhere.

She turned restlessly in the big bed, and finally reached over to her lamp and switched it on. A footstool by the high old bed helped her to get down. One leg felt asleep, stinging with the bites of thousands of invisible little teeth when she put her weight there. She paused to rub it, cursing for a moment the disadvantages of old age. When the legs were young and strong and supple you didn't appreciate the lack of pain. How could you when you had never felt pain? Something not experienced was not really known. How long would Ellen not know the nightmare that had plagued her most of her life was more than a nightmare?

But Tina? Surely not Tina, God in heaven, no, not Tina.

Just now when Lance had found someone to love. Someone who had built with him a dream. His father would have been so pleased to see small Crayley sons and daughters around the old ranch house again. If this thing that Ellen told her was right, then Lance's dream would turn to a nightmare far worse than Ellen's had ever been.

She took her rubber-tipped cane from the back of a chair and, using it to make up for the weakness in her shrunken legs, started walking. She got the flashlight from the drawer, and with it lighted her way into the hall. But then she snapped it off and walked slowly and quietly along the dark hall, the cane in her left hand, the flashlight in her right. At Lance and Tina's door, she paused for a moment but there was no sound. She wished she dared go in and shine the light in Tina's face and see for herself. She had not thought of it before.

Louise went on, trying to keep her steps soundless. At Ellen's door she paused too. A light shone under the door and a rustling of movement told her Ellen was still awake. At three-fifteen she was unable to sleep? No wonder she seemed more nervous lately, with darker shadows in her cheeks. Louise wished to call to her and tell her to keep her door blocked now, with a chair or a chest, or anything, when she slept and was defenseless. But it might prove useless, and serve only to frighten her more.

She went on to climb the third story stairs, using her flashlight now, going back up there for the first time in several years. She turned her light on the door to Ellen's old room, but she didn't go near it. She went instead to the door on her left, the small room where Mary Lou had lived. And she went in, closing the door behind her. The beam of the light showed her the deep gouges in the wood of the furniture, the holes in the carpet, and finally the wind chime in the corner. It was the only thing left that had in a way belonged to Mary Lou, and she wondered what Ellen had meant when she said they weren't right. Originally they had belonged to Irene. Given to her by someone from the carnival. An old gypsy fortune teller.

Louise sat down on a low chair, turned her light out and leaned her head against the back of the chair. She had almost forgotten Mary Lou. For her, too, the child had receded into a nightmare of the past.

If she concentrated, could she recall Mary Lou well enough to see her face again?

Louise's sons had both married women younger than themselves. With Albert it was a gypsy girl from a cheap traveling carnival. When he first brought Irene home, Louise felt she could never accept the marriage. Why hadn't he done like other men and married a nice, common local girl instead of a carnival transient? But he was already thirty and asked no one's opinion. His heart had gone out to the girl. She was beautiful true, but she was also one of the unfortunate. She even had an illegitimate child who lived in another state with the grandmother. The child of a rapist. A man who caught her in the dark of night and pulled her into the weeds of the roadside. She hadn't even seen his face.

After Albert's marriage to Irene, Louise came to like her, to admire the way she handled her life, even the household. When Ellen was born it seemed as if life on the Crayley ranch could get no better. Then when Ellen was eighteen months old, the grandmother of the illegitimate child died and Mary Lou came to the ranch to live. As long as Louise lived she would not forget the day. Irene had been gone a week, and the little girl who came home with her was about nine or ten years old. She resembled her mother only in that she too was dark. The diamond shape of her face added spark somehow to the piercing unfriendliness in her eyes. When she was spoken to, she spat. Irene, embarrassed, tried to urge her to be friendly, to apologize, but Mary Lou remained fiercely hostile.

The family dismissed it as rebellion against the death of her grandmother, with whom she had lived always, and Mary Lou was moved into the third story, across the hall from baby Ellen. Louise remembered her to be very quiet, hardly ever seen. She stayed in her room most of the time, and, they discovered, Ellen's room.

Ellen was about two years old the first time her screams brought the family running. They found the baby cornered, blood streaming from a series of jabs on her forearm and Mary Lou trying to smother the screams with one hand and striking at her with the blunt cut-out scissors held in her other hand. Mary Lou was dragged off, fighting, still silent. Irene grabbed up the baby and ran with her into her own room.

Of course the scissors were taken away. But then began the nightmare.

At night the baby would wake the household, screaming, and they would go to her room to find Mary Lou standing silently in a corner. She always denied doing anything.

Finally, Albert insisted the child be put away. Institutionalized. She was psychotic, he said. And Louise had thought he must be right. One day after an awful week during which Mary Lou had been especially destructive, when finally Ellen had to be guarded constantly, Irene made her decision. With tears in her eyes she told Louise, "Ellen is mine. I love her. But this other child is mine too and she has no one but me. I can't put her away, I would never rest. The only way I can protect Ellen is to take Mary Lou and leave. Ellen has you. That's far more than many children have. Albert tells me if I go, he will consider me dead. That he will tell Ellen I died. If it has to be that way, then it has to be that way. But this I promise you, and I promise Ellen, my baby. I will never allow Mary Lou to harm her."

The heartbreak of that day was still in Louise's heart. Albert closed himself in his office, and Ellen, not yet three years old, cried for her mother. When Albert came out of his office he went to another town, in another county, and bought the headstone, and then he sent away all household help for two weeks vacation. While they were gone he buried his life with Irene.

For many years Louise expected to hear from Irene again, but no word came. Finally she put her and her strange, destructive child out of her mind. To her relief, and in answer to her prayers, Ellen too forgot. Only in her dreams did she remember. Louise could see Mary Lou now, as plainly as if she stood before her.

A long sigh broke from her, and when she stood up she seemed more bent than before. Slowly she went downstairs, and on to the breakfast room where she waited for daylight, for Maud to start the day, for Tina. Maud, muttering something under her breath, pushed through the swinging doors with a loaded tray. She stopped short, her voice silenced long enough for Louise to say good morning without interruption. Then Maud collected her voice and went on to the table with the tray.

"You up already you must not have slept much ..." Her sharp eyes followed the lines of Louise's long flannel gown under a lace trimmed robe. "... or even dressed this morning—it's my idea you didn't sleep and I figured as much when you needed that milk after that fuss up there last night. I never did understand what Tina was doing in Ellen's room in the first place and it seemed to me it was Tina owed Ellen the apology instead of the other way around—she said she called her—Ellen I mean, and Ellen said she didn't. Anyway you're having a cold breakfast this morning with cereal and milk because that George hasn't shown up yet and if it was me running this place I'd fire him when ..."

"He isn't even hired, Maud. You can use the electric stove for cooking. And the electric coffee pot. And the toaster, of course."

Maud finished setting the table, including the toaster from the cupboard. "... he gets back it will be a good thing to have some kind of heat in this mausoleum ..." She disappeared into the hall, and her voice screeched back, "Breakfast!" and then she was back, talking on and on.

Louise had no appetite, but if she didn't force something down Maud wouldn't be able to stand it. She spent a long time preparing the slice of toast Maud handed her. She trimmed the crust away, spread butter and jam, and then broke it daintily, taking time to clean her fingers on her napkin. Then she sipped her coffee. By then footsteps and murmuring voices were in the hall outside. It was Lance and Tina at last, and Louise very carefully kept her eyes on her coffee. She answered their good mornings, and felt Tina's hands touch her shoulders, and her cool lips kiss her cheek lightly.

"How are you this morning, Mother Crayley?" the fine little voice asked. She went on around the table and sat down.

Louise raised her eyes. Her hand shook, rattling the spoon against the cup. Hastily she put it down and clasped her hands out of sight in her lap. Her own blindness amazed her now. Though the girl was seventeen years older, a grown woman, though her hair was bleached white and worn in an upsweep, though makeup concealed and camouflaged, the face was still the same.

Mary Lou had returned.

Louise looked down, wetting her lips with her tongue. She wondered about Irene, and knew she must have died. There was no other way that Mary Lou could have returned as she had. Oh Lance, you fool, you fool. But was Lance to be held responsible? How many times had he seen Mary Lou when she lived here? Twice, maybe. He was too young to have noticed her.

The breakfast ended, with Ellen a late arrival again. She looked tired and as tense as Louise felt.

Maud banged in from the kitchen bringing the newspaper. "Good thing the weather is warm or we'd freeze to death—here's your paper Louise I see that strike is still ..."

"I don't believe I'll read it just now," Louise said, standing, using her cane. "I think I'll go up and rest a while before I dress."

Tina had risen too, and came around the table to take her arm. "Let me help you, Mother Crayley." Her hand closed firmly on Louise's wrist. Louise resisted the urge to jerk away. The sharp black eyes smiled down at her. No, laughed at her. Delighted in fooling her. Maybe, Louise thought, it was just as well Tina help her upstairs. It would give her an opportunity to talk and to ask Tina what she wanted. Why she had come back pretending to be a stranger. She had even lied to Lance about her age. But of course she would have to. It was Mary Lou who was twenty-nine. Tina would have to change even that to avoid suspicion.

"Thank you," Louise said, but she leaned her weight on the cane.

In their slow progress up the stairs Louise wondered what to say to her. Whether to tell her outright she knew who she was, or to go along with the pretension until she could decide what to do. Oh, if only Albert were here, she found herself saying silently, if only Albert would come home. He had always handled their problems since his father had died and left him in charge.

They had reached her room and Tina said, "Let me help you to your bed."

"Thank you, I can manage now." She couldn't talk to Tina now. She wanted to be alone, to think. "If you'll just close the door for me …"

The door closed after a moment, and Louise looked back to make sure she was alone. She went to her bed and lay down, her eyes closed. What had Mary Lou come back for? What did she want? It had something to do with Ellen. Suddenly Louise was more afraid than she had ever been. For Ellen. What was she going to do to Ellen?

She had to get to the phone. She had to call Albert and tell him it was urgent that he come home. Then she had to tell Mary Lou — Tina—that she knew who she was. It might keep her from doing whatever she had come to do. Not until she reached the stairs did Louise remember her cane. She held to the bannister, feeling a wave of dizziness take her for a moment, then she went on, one slow step at a time, down to the main hall and along an adjacent hall to Albert's office and the telephone. She sat at the large old desk that had belonged to her husband's grandfather, and placed the call with the operator. Then she waited. It seemed hours before the phone rang. She lifted it quickly, hoping Maud hadn't heard the ring. The hotel proprietor told her in hard to understand English that Albert Crayley was not in, that he would be glad to take a message.

Louise had no choice. "Please tell him it's urgent that he call home." To make sure there was no mistake she gave her name and phone number.

She stayed by the phone, though she knew it might be hours, or even days. And she thought of Ellen, of a little girl who used to sit on her lap and say, "Tell me about my mother. What color was her hair?" She would answer, "The color of sunshine and gold. Now, if you'll bring me a book, we'll read a story." Anything to change the subject. And the nights a growing Ellen had run screaming to her room. Shaking, sobbing, the way she had when she was a baby and Mary Lou had been there and had done things to her that no one knew. Things that burned into the baby's subconscious, a face that remained to terrify her.

Then the night that Ellen, weeping, told her, "She wants to kill me. Why does she want to kill me? I just made her up out of my dreams and yet she wants to kill me."

Louise pushed away from the desk, got up, nervous, unable to sit still. She should dress, she thought. Be prepared. Prepared for what? She wasn't sure, but she felt it was vital that she dress. If the phone rang, Maud would answer it and call her. Of course she would. Mary Lou—Tina, *Tina—she must remember to call her Tina*—Tina wouldn't intercept the call. Which was the right way—to let Tina know she was fooling no one, or wait and let Albert handle it? Did she dare go to Lance? No. Lance was blind with calf-love, acting like a fifteen year old who had just discovered girls. Tina had handled him just right to accomplish her purpose which was, Louise had no doubt, to return to Crayley Ranch and somehow destroy Ellen. And then perhaps everything.

She went upstairs, dragging herself slowly along by the bannister. There was no lock on her door. On any interior door. She had never felt a need for one before. She dressed quickly, without pulling the bell rope for help. Only the large, old-fashioned master bedroom had a tasseled rope hanging down by the bed, handy to summon someone in the kitchen. Except for those years right after the stroke, she had never used it. Then she used it as little as possible because it made Maud nearly hysterical with surprise. It was always so unexpected.

The sound of an automobile brought Louise to a window to see who it was. Then she remembered George. Rodney had driven the jeep into the driveway by the house, and Ellen was going out to meet him. They stood halfway between jeep and house facing each other. Louise felt a softening in her heart, a gentle yearning for years gone by, years of her youth when she had been beautiful too in her way, and loved by a man as outstanding as Rodney. Rodney touched Ellen's arm as if he had to touch her, and Ellen reached one hand to brush back her wind-blown hair. Their talk seemed to be serious. Probably he had not found George. Louise drew a deep breath and turned away from the window.

The phone call—she had to be downstairs and ready to take it when it came.

This time she got her cane. She decided to go into the sitting room and try to read the paper. Lance was there, his feet up, the paper in his hands. Tina had the glass doors of the display cabinet open and was looking closely at an antique china doll. She had a feather duster under her arm. Yesterday Louise would have gone to stand beside her and give her the history on the old, old china doll. Today she saw in Tina's face—how it changed when she was not smiling—a greed too deep to ever satisfy. Louise sat down, watching her profile, the small tight mouth, the glowing dark eyes. She looked away quickly when Tina turned her way.

"Oh Mother Crayley," she said, smiling now. "I didn't hear you come in. You slip around as quietly as a kitten." She came over, and pulled an afghan from the back of a chair. "Here, darling, put your legs up and let me tuck you in. Want the TV on?"

Yesterday Louise ate up the phony softness and solicitous care. Today she cursed herself for being a fool. "I—not too loud, please." She had to be able to hear the phone. Tina hadn't waited to see if

Louise wanted to be tucked in, or wanted the TV on; she had gone on doing those things with a quickness like a bird building its nest.

"I guess you want your paper," Lance said lazily. "I'm in no hurry."

He tossed it onto her afghan-covered knees. "I'm through with it anyway. Come here, Childbride."

"I'm busy," Tina said curtly. "Why don't you go to work?"

Lance looked surprised. Then he laughed and shrugged. "I'll have to wait until my big brother comes home and tells me where I fit in."

"So why does he have to tell you? The ranch is yours too, isn't it? As well as everything else?"

Lance shrugged and looked at his mother. "To tell the truth I don't know how Dad's will left things."

So Tina was interested in the inheritance. Louise moistened her lips. "As long as I'm here ..." That somehow seemed the wrong thing to say. "Your father left everything to be shared equally by his sons, although Albert is the trustee."

The tightness left Tina's face and she smiled. "Then go get to work, Mister Crayley."

Louise thought Lance looked embarrassed. This was a side of Childbride he hadn't seen before.

The phone rang, a soft bell in the front of the house and the kitchen. Louise jumped, and Tina said, "I'll get it, Mother."

"No!" She hadn't intended being so shrill, but she was tangled in the afghan and desperate to keep Tina from the phone. Tina turned and looked at her, eyes sharp and steady, deep-set in their sockets, like the black stagnant water in a well. And Louise suddenly wondered what difference it would actually make if Tina did answer the phone. She sat back, gave up on disentangling herself. "That is—I was expecting a call."

Tina turned without answering and left the room.

Louise began again to put aside the afghan, her knotted hands trembling. "Help me with this, will you, Lance?"

"Sure."

In a moment she was free, tense and waiting.

Tina came back, saying, "It was for Ellen. Somebody wanted a date, I think. An old boyfriend. She turned him down." She went again to the glass display cabinet.

"Why'd she do that?" Lance asked lazily.

"Because," Tina said, and Louise saw the corners of her mouth turn down, "she's in love with the hired man, didn't you know that?"

There was too much contempt in her voice, and Louise felt indignant. "Rodney is a fine young man. He comes from a good family. He's well educated. More important, he has good character. He deserves the best."

"Which is Ellen," Tina said, her voice heavy with sarcasm. And then she opened her fingers and the china doll fell and shattered at her feet.

Louise gasped and reached out as if she might catch it. Then she sat dumbfounded, looking at the ruins of the most treasured antique of all.

Tina said, "I'm so sorry!" She stood with her head hanging, like a child crushed with remorse.

Lance hurried to her and put his hand on her shoulder. "Don't cry, Childbride; it was just an old doll. Not important."

He hadn't seen what she had seen then, Louise thought, still surprised, and yet wondering why. This was typical of Mary Lou—plain outright destruction. Why should she feel so surprised? Suddenly she was so angry she could hardly breathe.

"Not important? That doll belonged to your great-great grandmother, Lance. It was very old." She wanted to say more, but she was afraid she would say too much. She collected her cane from the floor and got up. "I'm going to help Maud awhile," she said.

She peeled potatoes. Home grown potatoes from George's

garden. Sometimes she listened to Maud. But mostly she listened for the phone and thought about Ellen and whether she should warn her to be on guard against Mary Lou—Tina. If she did, she would have to explain about the false grave, about the lies that had built up through the years because Albert had been afraid she would try to get in touch with her mother. Albert would be furious if she tried to explain that to Ellen, and he would be right because it was his business, not hers.

Maud's voice interrupted her thoughts. "Is something wrong, Louise? You'd stare a hole in those taters if they weren't so thick and when you act like that I can't help but think you're not feeling very well ..."

"I feel fine," Louise said, peeling furiously, making up her mind. She'd wait for Albert. Surely he would call before long. Though he may have gone out on that cattle ranch, and if he has there's no telling how long before he'll be back. "If Albert calls be sure to let me know. Even if it's three o'clock in the morning."

"Now why would he call at that hour when he knows you don't ..."

"The hours, I mean the time, is different there, I think. He might not remember."

"Albert? When Albert won't stop to think he'll be dead."

Louise shuddered involuntarily and nicked her finger with the knife. Maud was almost instantly at her side, taking from her the knife and the pan of potatoes.

"Here—see you hack yourself to pieces in my kitchen is not what I'm here for now hold your finger in this pan of water until I can get a bandage ... "

"It's not that bad, Maud, for gracious sakes!"

"... and get you fixed up—if you want to sit in here and talk that's fine but you leave the work to me I ..."

· · ·

THE PHONE DIDN'T RING. At lunch Louise forced a few bites of food down for Maud's benefit. She noticed that Ellen was doing the same. Ellen's lovely eyes looked larger than ever and shadowed. The dip below her cheek bones seemed deeper. Louise kept looking at her; when Ellen noticed, she smiled.

"Granny, is there something I can get for you?"

"No, dear. Thank you. I guess Rodney didn't find George, or you would have told us. "

Ellen's smile faded, and she looked down. "No, he hasn't found him. Rodney is really worried. So am I."

Louise felt a twinge of conscience. She had been so concerned with her own problems that George being unexplainably gone had almost slipped her mind. She touched her forehead with her hand. "I must be getting old," she said.

They all looked at her a little strangely, and she started to say something, anything, that would make sense of it when she was interrupted by the ringing of the phone. Its suddenness nearly stopped her heart. She knocked over her cup as her hands flew to her chest. Ellen got up and came around the table to help her, and Maud, pausing long enough to see that Ellen needed no help, went toward the kitchen to answer the phone.

Lance said, "You seem awfully nervous today, Mother, aren't you feeling well?"

Louise heard him, but she didn't answer right away because she was seeing the look on Tina's face. It was a look of suspicion, perhaps even understanding. Maud called Ellen to the phone, and Tina rose as if to take her place.

"I believe Mother Crayley is tired," Tina said, coming to lay cold hands on Louise's shoulders. "Let me help you up to your room."

Louise got her cane and rose. The walk along the central hall to the front stairs, and up, along that hall to Louise's front room, was a long walk, and a very slow walk that required patience. They went in silence, Tina's hand lightly under Louise's arm, no help to her whatsoever. Louise wondered what Tina was thinking, and wished she dared ask. Wished she knew how to handle it. She thought maybe it might help to tell Tina she knew, and would give her just so long to get out of the house. But her courage was as weak as her body and the thought of saying anything shook her like last year's leaf in the wind.

Tina finally broke the silence, just as they entered her room. "You're trembling, Mother dear." And it seemed to Louise her voice was contemptuous. She knew without looking that Tina was smiling. "I think you got too anxious waiting for that call. You did say you were waiting for a call, didn't you?"

"Yes, I said that," Louise replied stiffly. She didn't look up. She dropped her cane by the bed and sat back in her chair, the old chair that had sagged to fit her body. She closed her eyes, sighed, and said, "Please close the door when you go out."

The footsteps made hardly a sound on the overlapping profusion of rugs Louise had collected through the years, and the door, closing, was scarcely louder. The first feeling was one of relief that she was gone; the second sudden terror that she had not left the room at all, but stood there yet, her lips curled in the old way, taunting. Louise's eyes flew open. But instead of being by the door, Tina stood within reach, laughing silently down at her.

Louise thought for a moment she would faint, but the moment passed with only the smallest moan of fright escaping her tight throat. Her heart pounded, beating in her ears like big rubber hammers.

Tina's voice hissed in a loud whisper. "You're afraid of me! That's what I thought. I could see the change in you. Because of that silly doll?"

"No. Not because—of the—doll." Louise paused only to breathe more evenly. "What do you want here?"

A long silence answered her. Tina's laughter, and all pretense, had gone. Her eyes were narrow and hard, calculating. Her mouth pinched. Louise decided to go on with it.

"I know who you are. I don't know what you want here. I'm sure that you didn't marry Lance for love, you married him because of who he is. But, what is it you want, Mary Lou?"

The small mouth came untied and opened slowly. "How did you know me?" she asked.

"You haven't changed that much. You can change the covering, but you can't change your skeleton. Your face is the same. When you aren't smiling you look exactly the way you used to. "

"But with a difference, Granny. Now I'm a big girl. And now I have a right here. It took me months to find that bachelor son of yours and get him to marry me, but I did it. You can't kick me out this time, Granny."

"We didn't kick you out ..."

"Oh yes. Oh yes, you did, in your smug little way."

"Your mother took you, Mary Lou, because she felt it was better that way."

"I know what she did. I wasn't so stupid. You were going to lock me up. You think I didn't know? Just because of that crummy room. If you had given me the room I wanted, I wouldn't have messed it up."

"But that was Ellen's room. And it wasn't because of the room, Mary Lou, and you know it." There was no point in arguing, Louise thought, and changed to a question. "Where is Irene now, Mary Lou?"

"Call me Tina!" She swung about, angrily, went to the chest of drawers and began to look through it in a slow and casual manner, just as she had as a child. A vicious, meddlesome brat, one of the maids had called her.

"All right. Tina. Where is your mother?"

"She's dead." There was no emotion in her voice.

Louise felt the truth in the statement. "I'm sorry. I was very fond of Irene. What happened?"

Tina turned and looked at Louise, evidently watching for the effect her words would have. "I got tired of her telling me what to do all the time and I killed her."

Though from Mary Lou one could expect statements and actions intended to shock, still Louise couldn't help the jolt it gave her. "Why do you say things like that, Mary Lou!"

Tina's amusement ended. "I said don't call me that! No one has called me that since we left here. Mother changed our names. So stop doing it! I am Tina. *Tina.*" She leaned down into Louise's face, so near Louise turned her own face away. "Tina. Tina. Tina. And, I might add, Tina Crayley." She straightened and turned away, looking around the room. "Which is what I should have been all the time. You see, Granny, I just came into my rightful inheritance."'

Louise stared at her, watched her sample perfume on the dressing table. "Why, what do you mean by that? Your name is—was ..." She couldn't remember. It had been something quite common but now she couldn't even remember.

Tina whirled, flashes of dark anger coming to surface in her strange eyes again. "Not *my* name. I had no name. But when my mama married, then I had a name! And it was Crayley. Why should Ellen get my name? Why was she born? Why should she have gotten the things that are rightfully mine? Nobody takes what is mine—not then, not ever, and gets by with it. I have come back, just as I always planned to, to take what is mine. She tried to stop me, but she couldn't. She should never have tried to stop me."

Louise spoke before she thought, a whispered remark. "You're insane."

Tina shook her head and laughed. "No. You're still wrong. I have no problem. You're the one with the problem. I'm as capable of taking care of myself in this world as anyone."

"Then go—get out," Louise said, her voice unsteady. "Because if you're still here when Albert ... "

"So he's the one you called! My dear, long lost father. He can't do anything now, Granny, because Lance is my husband. It's all up to Lance. And he will never do anything I don't want him to. It took me several months to get him to marry me, but now all he cares about is me." Laughing, twisting her body, she went out and slammed the door soundly.

It was good to hear. Louise wished again for a lock, then gave in to the flush of weakness brought on by her pounding heart, her anger, and her fear. There was nothing to do now but wait. Wait for Albert to call, to come home.


TINA's angered outburst about what she felt was hers brought back a stream of memories. The day Irene had left, at last pulling the child forcibly while she clung screaming to the bannister. The third story had been hers, she had felt, and once again Louise ached under the helpless indecision. Were they wrong? Because like a feline Mary Lou's passion was for things, not people; were they treating her unfairly? Were they wrong? *Leave Mary Lou up there and leave her alone, and she'll be all right.* How many times had she said that? And at last, *take the baby out, take her away where Mary Lou can't reach her. Or, for God's sake, get psychiatric help for the child. Before she kills the baby.*

Irene had shown fair and impartial judgment in all things but that. And it was then Irene told her that ridiculous story. She remembered it now almost word for word. And it stunned her as much as it had then.

"A doctor would do no good. You see, though I bore Mary Lou, she does not belong to me or anyone. She is a descendant of Bast, the cat goddess. When she was born we saw the difference, Mama and I. She was very weak, and she mewed like a kitten. She was dying. So Mama got this old gypsy woman who knew everything, and the minute she saw the baby she backed out of the trailer. Outside she told Mama that the baby was only partially human, and there was nothing we could do. Let her die, she said. Much better to let her die, because her mind will never be like human minds and no one will understand her. But we loved her and didn't want her to die, so she said she'd see if there was anything to be done. In a few days the old woman brought the wind chime. She had made it herself and put magic in it. Hang it and never let it break, she said, and she will live, but if the chime should break she will die ..."

The story stunned Louise, not because she believed it, but because Irene, who had seemed to be so sensible, believed it. When Louise objected, Irene still refused the doctor.

"Then I'll guard her myself," Irene had said, "forever if I have to, to keep her away from the baby. I'll guard her myself—forever ..."

Louise shook her head, her brain as heavy as her heart. "Only you couldn't, could you, Irene?" she said aloud. And then she went to her bed and lay down.

In the end, the day when Irene finally left, she managed to control Mary Lou and get her to go willingly only by leaving the chime hanging in the bedroom. To Mary Lou the chime was important and should stay where she could not. Louise had forgotten the old thing was still in the house until Ellen mentioned it.

LOUISE DIDN'T GO DOWN for dinner. Maud brought soup to her bed. Ellen came and helped her into her nightgown. Louise started to tell Ellen to be careful, to tell her who Tina really was. But then she remembered the empty grave, and the lies. She was so tired. "If only I could rest," she said. "It's awful to be old and worn out and still be unable to rest."

"Should I call the doctor, Granny?"

"No, mercy no. All I need ..." She stopped, thinking of the rest of her intended statement. *All I need is to hear from Albert. To get something done. I don't know what.*

"Your medicine? The nerve medicine, so you can sleep?"

Louise started to say yes, then remembered that she must be able to talk to Albert when he called. "No, not the medicine, just rest."

. . .

Her sleep that night was pierced by dreams of baby Ellen, less than two years old, screaming in her crib, clawed welts on her face turning angry purple—and by the ringing of the telephone. When she roused herself and listened, the house was quiet, creaking in its old age like herself. There was no phone ringing, no baby crying. She dozed again and dreamed Ellen entered her room and came to stand by her bed. When she woke and turned she saw the figure there, only faintly outlined by the pale light that came through the curtains at her windows. She started to sit up, but the figure moved nearer. A hand touched her shoulder and pushed her back. The hand was small and soft and cold as death.

She gasped to scream when the pillow came down over her face, closing her into the prison of no light, no air. She clawed at the hands that held the pillow, at the knees that pushed against her, pinioning her body to the bed. But mostly she clawed at the air she could not reach. Into the small remaining consciousness of her mind came the final words:

"You asked why I came here, Granny. I'll tell you. I came to kill Ellen, and *nobody* is going to stop me."

# CHAPTER 6

"Ellen! Ellen, wake up, for the Lord's sake, wake up!"

The voice came down the hall accompanied by running steps. Ellen was awake and sitting on the side of her bed by the time the door flew open, Miss Maud behind it. Miss Maud's eyes were round as cups and about to overflow.

"It's your granny," she said, "Ellen ..." Her chin began to jerk and she held it tight, puckered, her voice silent. She just stood there staring at Ellen, the tears finally running over.

Ellen ran. By the time she reached her grandmother's room Lance was already there, holding the limp, wrinkled hand. Calling her. At the foot of the bed stood Tina.

Lance ordered in a nervous voice, "Go call a doctor." Tina turned, going out of the room. Then Lance raised his eyes. "Ellen, she's already cold." He looked like a little boy who had just discovered a terrible truth about life.

Ellen walked to the bed slowly. As she took Granny's hand she thought that must be the worst part, the coldness. Here was her grandmother, really the only mother she had ever known, and yet she was gone. There was an ambivalence in it that she could not grasp. It was beyond her to understand it. The suddenness of death. The fact of it. The mystery. And the reason. She kept sitting there, the cold hand unmoving in hers. Miss Maud came into the room. Tears now instead of words. And Tina came back. Then a doctor came. He made Ellen let go the hand and leave the room.

"Go downstairs," he said. "Get some coffee. Some food." As if he knew Miss Maud and her position he said, "Cook some breakfast. Or lunch."

They all went down to the kitchen and stood around. After awhile Miss Maud put coffee on the electric stove. Ellen noticed the old iron cookstove that usually ate coal like a caterpillar eating leaves stood cold and untouched. No fire had been built anywhere. And she was still in her pajamas without even a robe.

Tina touched her. "Sit down, Ellen, and let me bring you some toast. We'll all feel better if we eat. There are things to be done. You'll want the men to know, won't you? I'll go ask Rodney to come to the house."

"Thank you," Ellen said, sitting as she had been told, accepting the toast Tina brought, though not eating it. Tina kissed Lance, and went out the back door.

"She's worth her weight in diamonds, Childbride is," said Lance.

Ellen saw that his eyes were misted, looking at the door through which she had gone. He didn't seem to expect an answer, and she didn't feel like giving one. She thought of Rodney coming in soon now, and of herself in wrinkled pajamas. Instinct sent her to her room in search of a robe.

She decided to dress while she was there, to wash her face and brush her hair. As a result Rodney was already in the kitchen being served coffee by Tina when Ellen returned. He met her near the door and pressed her hands between his.

"You're icy. The whole house is icy. I'll get one of the boys to build some fires. Ellen, I'm sorry about your grandmother."

"Thank you, Rodney."

Tina said, "Come have some coffee, Ellen. It will help warm you."

The doctor came into the kitchen then, and began to ask questions and to explain, pausing to thank Tina when she brought him a cup of coffee. "She seems to have passed peacefully in her sleep," he said. "I don't know her history. Has she been sick? Of course when a person is that old ..."

Ellen shook her head. "Not especially sick. She wasn't strong, of course. She'd had a stroke years ago. Doctor Woodard was her doctor. I forgot to tell Uncle Lance."

Lance said, "She told me she was having trouble with her heart."

The doctor nodded. "That was it, probably. You might like to call her regular doctor in."

Lance shook his head. "What's the point? What do we do now?"

Rodney said, "For one thing we call Mr. Crayley home." He looked at Ellen as he spoke. "I'll call from the ranch office, and get those fires started."

The doctor shivered visibly. "It is extremely cold in here. Much colder than it is outside, in fact, it's ..." He stopped, and Ellen saw his eyes take in the high, dark ceiling, the few narrow windows. But he didn't say what he was thinking.

Lance mumbled something about central heating, and the doctor prepared to leave.


WHEN THE AMBULANCE came to take the body away, Ellen wondered who had thought to call them. Tina probably, who seemed suddenly to be thinking of everything. It was she who told what rooms to heat, and she who thought to bring meat from the freezer to cook. Ellen was glad to be free to go to her room, now warm, and let Tina take care of the house.

Her father arrived home about ten o'clock the following morning. He drove a white Cadillac, his trademark. He had left it parked at the airport, waiting for his return. He came in looking exactly as he had when he'd gone away. Albert Crayley had never been a smiling man anyway, that Ellen could remember. And sunshine seemed to have little effect on his pale skin. He kissed Ellen's cheek, nodded at Miss Maud, and shook Lance's hand.

"Good to see you again, Lance. Sorry it had to be under these conditions."

Lance nodded and pulled Tina forward. Ellen wondered if he would refer to her as Childbride now, and doubted it. For the first time she noticed the change in Tina's makeup and hairdo. Her hair was still in an upsweep, but bangs had been freed and fell almost to her eyes. Her makeup too was darker. It looked almost as if she intended to camouflage herself.

"This is my wife, Tina," Lance said. "She's been just great. She's been thinking of all the things the rest of us have forgotten. Like dinner, for instance."

Albert took Tina's hand in his. "Welcome to the family, Tina. We're glad to have you. I'm glad Mother got a chance to meet you before she passed away."

"Thank you, Mr. Crayley. I was happy to know Mother Crayley too. We've waited for you. Lance thought you would like to make funeral arrangements."

"Yes. But call me Albert, please."

"Thank you. If you'll excuse me I'll go help Miss Maud."

She smiled, backed away, and went down the hall toward the kitchen. Ellen went with her father and uncle into her father's office.

"We'll bury her here, of course," Albert said. "On the hill, in the family cemetery, beside Papa. I'll go in and choose the coffin. What was wrong?"

Ellen sat back, quiet, letting the men do the talking. That was the way it was in her family. Male dominated. So far as the men could tell. Actually, she could remember that Granny had ruled undercover, and sometimes not so undercover. At least about some things.

"Natural causes, the doctor said."

"Natural causes? How natural?" Her father's voice sounded suddenly angry. "And what doctor?"

"Uh—I think he must be fairly new, he's young. Tina called him." Lance looked at Ellen. "I don't remember his name, do you?"

She answered, "I'm sure we can find out if it's necessary."

Her father had paced from desk to fireplace and back. He was more agitated than Ellen had ever seen him. Of course his mother had just died. She supposed he was as upset as any of them; it was just that she expected him to be the calm, firm person he had always been.

"I'll have Doctor Woodard to check with him anyway. There was something wrong. What was it?" He looked at both of them, Ellen first.

"Wrong?" Lance answered.

"Damnit yes! She was sick and neither of you knew it?"

They returned his stares, Ellen biting her lower lip.

"No, she didn't tell me," Ellen said.

Albert straightened and got himself under control. "When I returned to the hotel, there was a message waiting for me. Mother had called several hours earlier than Rodney, saying it was extremely urgent that I get in touch with her. She had even asked that someone be sent after me. Don't either of you know what was wrong?"

This time neither of them answered. Ellen stared at her father. For Granny to call a man in from his work was unthinkable. Granny's lifetime job had been to protect the men from household problems.

"Unfortunately," her father continued, "I had not left enough information at the hotel for them to find me. I hadn't planned to be gone more than twenty-four hours, and I wasn't sure exactly where I'd be. Just somewhere in the country, of course. I suppose you're both aware that Mother has never done anything like this before. And yet neither of you were aware of anything being wrong?" He seemed to find it incredible, and Ellen tried to think back over the day preceding her grandmother's death.

"She did seem more tired than usual, and nervous. She didn't even come down for supper."

Lance said, "She was irritable all day. She was cranky as hell with Tina when she accidentally broke—a little thing."

"I'm sorry I didn't spend more time with her," Ellen said. "But I didn't know—she ..."

Albert came to her and patted her shoulder. "It can't be helped now. Why she didn't tell you, we'll never know. I'll go in now to the funeral home and see what has to be done."

They followed him from his office and stood for a moment in the hall, indecisive, troubled. Lance wandered off then, in search of Tina, Ellen supposed. She was glad to be alone. She went slowly upstairs to Granny's room. The bed was still unmade, the comforters thrown back, the small depression in the bottom sheet showing how incredibly small Granny's body had become in her old age. A mere eighty pounds for several years now. Ellen went to the bed and touched the thick, soft pillow. It hurt to know that Granny had desperately needed someone and she had not known.

She used the footstool to boost herself up and sat on the edge of the big bed, her cheek resting against the cool dark wood of the headboard. She would not have seen the alien thing on the bed if her hand had not touched it. Small and sharp and hard, it poked into the palm of her hand. She picked it up, rolling it between her fingers. A tiny, clear crystal bead, with a tiny broken wire on one point. Puzzled, she looked at it closely under the lamp. It had been a part of inexpensive costume jewelry, such as Granny had never owned. Not, at least, to Ellen's knowledge. Tina wore earrings. But what would Tina's broken earring be doing under a pillow on Granny's bed? Another possibility was the men who had come to take the body out on the stretcher, or the doctor. It could be a part of something that was not jewelry at all. She got down from the bed and lay the tiny crystal in a small carved catchall on a nearby chest, then she went to her own room.

Miss Maud's Indian summer didn't last long. The day of the funeral was gray, windy, and very cold. Tina was bundled into a beautiful fur coat, of rich, dark beaver. Ellen looked at it, admired it, and held her tongue on her opinion of people who bought animal fur. It seemed primitive and savage to slaughter an animal only for his coat. Her own coat was made of lamb's wool, which at least left the lamb intact to grow more wool.

Of course she had to admit that Tina annoyed her anyway, the way she had taken it on herself to change and rearrange the old Crayley home even before its mistress was buried. The day before, she had gone back to Granny's room to find that Tina had stripped the bed and emptied everything, even the carved catchall, and put away in boxes all of Granny's medicine, colognes and small personal things. Ellen looked for the tiny crystal, found it gone and asked Tina about it. Tina shrugged.

"I'm sorry, I guess I threw it away. What was it? Was it important?"

There wasn't anything Ellen could do, so she left the room. To object about the room being cleaned seemed childish. Still, Tina's presumptuousness irritated her.

Rodney stood on one side of her and her father on the other. Beside Rodney stood Tina, and then Lance. The hired men were there. Miss Maud was there. Beside the coffin stood the minister. The funeral parlor had been crowded with people, but none of them had come on to Crayley's Hill.

Ellen lowered her head against the wind and the bits of snow that were coming in now from the north and watched as the coffin was lowered into the ground and covered. Then she turned her back to the wind; but instead of following her father and uncle and the others back toward the house she moved closer to her mother's grave. The bulge was still there. It wasn't something she had imagined. Her mother's grave looked almost as recent as her grandmother's.

The voice in her ear said, "Ellen, don't you want to go in now? You'll freeze."

She looked up into Rodney's eyes. "Rodney ..." She wasn't sure what she wanted to ask.

"What is it?" he urged. He stood against her left shoulder, warm, shutting off the wind. She motioned with one gloved hand. "That grave over there is my mother's grave, Rodney. Shouldn't it be flatter than that?"

He didn't answer. She looked up after a moment to see that his narrowed eyes were examining the grave.

"So that's her grave," he said finally.

"Yes. I used to come here a lot. And I never noticed before that it wasn't flat like the others. Rodney, I'm sure it was. What could be wrong with it?"

His big hand closed over her arm. "Blowing sand can do odd things. Come on now and get out of this weather, before you get sick."

She let him guide her away, but she noticed that he looked back over his shoulder, and she knew he was still thinking about the grave. He didn't really believe that the wind had changed the shape of it. He opened the door for her, kissed her forehead and said, "Bye-bye little girl. See you. I've got some work to do." She didn't try to hide her disappointment, her feeling of crushing loneliness. But he had already turned away and gone out. She sagged against the wall. Another afternoon in this house without Granny seemed more than she could take. If it weren't for being away from Rodney she would go back to Denver.

She drew a long breath of resignation and went upstairs, slowly, watching her own feet. And thinking. Her mother's grave looked as if it were slowly rising. She had thought that the first time, and she thought it yet. But the thought disturbed her and she forced her mind away from it. She would simply have to find something with which to keep busy to avoid such morbid and impossible thoughts. First, a ghost in the third story, now a rising grave. She would be ashamed for anyone to know.

The funeral of her grandmother, or the arrival of her father, evidently had put an end to the new heating system. At least for the time. She found the usual bucket of coal beside her door. She took it in with her, found her room warm in comparison to the long, dark, frigid hall. The sound of the storm closed her in from the rest of the world. Denver, and the freedom it offered, seemed a long way off. The hours dragged, going from dim and dreary storm-controlled afternoon to dark and cold storm-controlled night. Then again into another day, snow blowing hard against her window, obscuring even the bunkhouse.

The old house made odd noises—cracking, popping, groaning, almost as cold inside as out, with only a few rooms heated, as always. Though Ellen's room was warm, the hall outside was still cold. Was always cold. Would always be cold. So it was a choice between her bedroom and the kitchen with Miss Maud. Lance and Tina had the sitting room, her father his office. She didn't feel like intruding on the privacy of any of them. Besides, if Rodney came to the house, he would come to the kitchen first.

Miss Maud continued to sniff, going nervously from stove to sink to refrigerator to table, to closet for dust pan and brush, or mops to take up what she spilled.

"... going wrong in this house so help me or already gone wrong and I'll swear the house has been changed because it's darker and it's colder and it's different ..."

Ellen sat on the kitchen stool and automatically reached for the salad bowl to help Miss Maud. "It's different because Granny's gone, Miss Maud." She bit her lips, swallowing the lump that rose to choke her. She thought of the third story, but she didn't speak of it to Miss Maud.

"Yes but there are other things too like the awful cold and that old man George missing and the house just keeps getting colder."

"Nobody can keep fires like Mr. Miller."

But Miss Maud had stopped to stare at her old iron cook-stove, and answered absently. "It's more than that. I keep the coal in there and I keep it full but the heat just goes up the chimney and I have to wear sweaters and I say there's something in this house that's just not normal anymore."

Ellen looked up, seeing on the windows at the end of the kitchen the beat of the winter storm, feeling the cold move along her arms, even under the thick, soft cashmere sweater. "The kitchen is cold today. But it doesn't seem right somehow, to go ahead with a heating system with Granny just ..."

She faltered, and stopped, and Miss Maud began to move again, going to a cabinet to bring down a fresh loaf of her home-made bread, and to a drawer for her favorite knife. "No, of course it wouldn't ..." she said, tossing cutlery around in the drawer. "... we've stood it before we can stand it again but I swear I must be blind today as well as cold because I can't ... "

"Would you like a vacation, Miss Maud? Maybe you'd like to go south for the winter."

"... find—that's what Tina suggested already she said to me this morning that I could have three months' vacation with pay and it ..."

"What?" Ellen's voice was sharper than she intended. "I mean, it isn't that you don't deserve it, Miss Maud, but who gave Tina authority to do that? I can hardly see father ..."

"sounded good—well that's what I thought too and I guess I said so because she puffed up like a Dominicker hen and said that now she was mistress of this house and she didn't need anybody to tell her what she could do so I just told her I reckoned I'd stay because I didn't feel that way about it, I mean I didn't tell her I didn't feel she had that much authority yet because I could see she wouldn't like it one whit but as long as Louise is not here then I figure—now where in the dickens is my knife? I had it right here—I dried it last night and put it in this drawer just the way I always do." She jerked the drawer out and turned it bottom side up on the cabinet. Knives, forks, long-handled spoons cluttered out. Her hand flipped through them and one by one began to place them back into the drawer. Ellen had left her stool to look over Miss Maud's shoulder.

"Maybe someone took it to slice bread for a snack," Ellen suggested.

"When? I've been here in the kitchen off and on since before daybreak and nobody ..."

"Sometime in the night, maybe."

"I would have heard because I always leave my bedroom door open ..." She stopped suddenly, staring at the wall, her mouth open. "I nearly forgot—that's another odd thing when I got up this morning my door was shut and I didn't shut it."

"Well, maybe Uncle Lance came down for a sandwich, saw your door was open and shut it so you wouldn't be disturbed. Maybe he left it on the table, or put it in another drawer."

"If he did he makes about as much noise as a ghost because I didn't hear a thing and I'm a light sleeper; I always hear George come in with the coal ..." She was moving, looking, searching for the knife. Ellen joined the search.

"George," Ellen said, "makes as much racket as a horse. Not that you aren't a light sleeper, of course."

"... no matter how early it is—I guess I'll just have to use something else for now but it's got to be here somewhere because knives don't just up and walk away."

Ellen went down the hall to the dining room and set the table. Though a fire burned energetically in the grate, the room seemed colder than it ever had. Ellen stood for a moment looking at the fire, thinking about Miss Maud's belief that the house was growing colder.

She heard nothing, but a feeling that someone stood just behind her brought her around, her stomach tightening in fear.

Tina stood at the end of the table staring at her. The deep-set, dark eyes held a hostility that made Ellen forget the sudden fright of having someone come to stand silently behind her. A smile touched Tina's small mouth. "You didn't hear me come in?"

"No, I didn't. I just wasn't expecting anyone, I guess."

"I see you have the table all set."

"Yes. I always have helped Miss Maud a little. She said you offered her a long vacation. I was wondering if you had someone else in mind to take her place. "

"Not particularly." She shivered, hugging her arms. "God, it's cold in this house. If Lance weren't starting to work in your dad's real estate office tomorrow, I'd make him take me somewhere where it's not so damned cold."

"Uncle Lance is going to work here?"

"Yes." Tina was on her way out, and glanced back over her shoulder. "You see I'm making an honest man out of him. I'm sure when he married me he didn't suspect I'd try. I think a man should earn his money."

Ellen looked after her, and continued to look at the doorway through which she had gone. Tina kept surprising her. At times she seemed frivolous and selfish. And then she came up with things like this, as if her determination to stick it out on the ranch was the most important thing in the world. Maybe Granny was right, and Tina would make a responsible man of Uncle Lance; would, in fact, remain here to become the mistress of Crayley mansion and be all that Granny had wanted in a daughter-in-law.

Ellen got the napkins from the buffet and finished the table. A whisper of a wish that Granny could be here to see this change in her household and family was swept aside in the fresh realization that Granny was now dead.

Miss Maud didn't pause to eat with the family. She was still looking for her knife.

"I want to know who took my knife," she demanded in a record-short sentence as she served the meat. "Did any of you come in and use my knife last night?" Everyone looked up at her but no one answered. Ellen glanced from her dad to Uncle Lance and saw them both stare at Miss Maud blankly. They didn't know what she was talking about. Miss Maud threw up her hands in disgust and went out of the room, muttering, leaving the meat platter on the table.

The storm blew away during the night and Ellen woke to find the sun shining. She looked out her window and saw the mountains brilliant white against a clear blue sky, and felt lifted, as if something about her was a part of it. How Granny had loved seeing new snow on the mountains.

She turned away from the mountain view and wondered how she would fill her day. She still had many odds and ends upstairs in her old bedroom. With the sun shining, the fear she'd had of the upper story seemed silly. There was no reason why she couldn't go up and bring down small keepsakes, old treasures. If she could find a box or an empty clothes basket, she could at least fill most of her day by lugging the rest of her things downstairs.

She ate breakfast alone, and because she was alone she ate in the kitchen. Her breakfasts never amounted to much. A small piece of dry toast and a tiny glass of fruit juice. Afterwards, coffee. Miss Maud was still grumbling about her knife and stopped only to answer Ellen's question about the rest of the family.

"I don't know anything about those people, I don't have time to watch out after them what with all the work there is to do and trying to locate that knife but I think Albert took Lance along with him when he went to town and is starting him right in on an eight to five day to work at the bank and Tina who knows where she is, she flies around here like a summer moth so that you never know where she is from one minute to the next; this house is still as cold as a tomb even with the sun shining but no wonder the sun never comes in ..."

"I'm moving today," Ellen said. "Do you have a clothes basket I can use?"

"... these little bitty narrow windows—clothes basket? Of course I have clothes baskets, Lord knows you need them around here—where are you moving to?"

"Downstairs, from my old room."

"The baskets are in the laundry room as always, I can help you if you need me—I don't guess there's much use spending any more time looking for that knife, I can't for the life of me figure out what could have happened to it ..."

"I can manage, thank you. I need something to do." When she reached the top floor and went into her room she found it dark and cold, the heavy draperies drawn across the window. She hadn't closed them, and went to push them back, far back: She had never liked them closed.

The couple standing together in the meadow at the foot of Crayley Hill drew her attention completely. Though they were far away Tina's blonde hair and dark brown coat were unmistakable. So too was Rodney. Ellen's body tensed and her throat grew dry and tight as she watched Rodney's arm go around Tina's waist. They turned and began walking slowly across the snow-spotted meadow. Then Tina's face turned up to him and they stopped again. It seemed to take forever for their lips to meet. The entire act seemed in slow motion. Her gloved hand up to his face, his face down to hers.

Ellen jerked the draperies together and turned her back to the window. She didn't want to see, or think, or feel. But no matter how tightly she closed her eyes the image was there—Rodney kissing Tina, as he had never kissed her. Was this why Tina had insisted Lance go to work? Ellen suddenly wondered if Tina and Rodney had known each other before.

She sat on her bed in the darkened room, hurting inside as if part of herself was being torn away. She had told Miss Maud she was moving. What was to keep her from literally moving out now? Now that Rodney ... She had her own car, her own money. But she couldn't leave without saying goodbye to her dad. Tomorrow maybe, she would go. Today, to keep busy, she would move her things downstairs. In the top drawer of an old chest was her collection of tiny blown glass animals. It was a collection started by her grandmother years before she was born, and passed on to her. Even as a child she had been very careful to not break any of it, which was why it had been packed in cotton in the drawer. She opened the drawer and found it empty.

She stared dully at the box-like interior of the drawer, her mind still numb with what she had seen out the window but coming slowly to grasp this strange circumstance. Who would empty her drawer of figurines? After a few minutes of trying to puzzle it out, of looking into other drawers, even into the closet shelves, she started downstairs to ask Miss Maud. But when she reached the bottom of the first flight of stairs she paused, her eyes going to the partly open door of Tina and Lance's room. As if her feet moved without conscious will, she went slowly along the hall to the door and pushed it open. Here too the draperies were drawn, and the room was almost as dark as the hall.

The figures were in plain sight, arranged neatly on the dresser in front of the mirror, their rainbow of colors sparkling even in the gloomy dark. Ellen crossed the room slowly and stood looking down at them, astounded at Tina's nerve. To explore the bedrooms was one thing, but to bring this out, and evidently take it for her own, was another. Ellen looked at other items on the dresser, and saw a tray of earrings. And among them a crystal earring with one broken prong. It lay in plain sight. Almost as if Tina wanted it seen. The broken section lay nearby. That was the part Tina had said she knew nothing about.

Ellen withdrew, closing the door, standing against it a moment, wondering, confused. It was too much to assimilate. Tina with Rodney, Tina taking the figurines, Tina lying about the earring ...

Her mind fighting against the increasing duplicity of Tina, Ellen went down to the sitting room. Here it was fairly warm and light. Here she felt closer to Granny and the uncomplicated life she had always known. She wondered what to do about the glass animals. Demand their return? Somehow it seemed a childish thing to do. Could she demand Rodney's return too? She tried to laugh at the analogy, but the attempt became a choke and a sob, and she put her head down on her arms and wept quietly. Her world was changing so fast that it was destroying everything she loved.

She didn't see Tina until her father and Uncle Lance came home and joined her in the dining room for dinner. Lance acted as if he hadn't seen his childbride for six months, and talked so much that even Miss Maud was silent when she brought the dessert in. Ellen too was silent. She had thought she would mention the figurines to Tina, but she was glad now to put it off until another time, when they were alone. But that too she did not search out. She found herself instead avoiding any contact with Tina, which was easy, since Tina seemed to be spending most of her time with Rodney.

It was less than a week after her grandmother's funeral that the sheriff came. Ellen looked out the window in the afternoon and saw the car parked in the driveway, Rodney standing with two uniformed men. They talked earnestly and then walked together down to the bunkhouse and to the barns. Ellen wondered where Tina was if not with Rodney. She brushed her hair, checked her makeup, and went down to the kitchen. Miss Maud was standing at the west window, the curtain pulled aside so as to see better. Then she saw Ellen.

"That's the sheriff out there, what on earth do you suppose the sheriff's here for unless it's something about George being found—oh, here they come." She dropped the curtain, straightened her apron and ran for the kitchen sink. She then searched nervously for something to do.

Ellen smiled. "If I didn't know you better, Miss Maud, I'd think you were very guilty about something."

"Oh dear I don't know a thing about ..." She went to answer the light knock at the kitchen door, which was unnecessary as Rodney had already opened it.

Ellen felt his unyielding gaze on her, but avoided looking into it. There was the sheriff and his deputy to speak to, to invite in for coffee and rolls.

"No thank you, Miss Crayley. We'd just like to ask a few questions about George Miller. The last time any of you saw him."

It was hard to remember. "There has been so much confusion lately, with the death of my grandmother, my father coming home, the funeral. I don't even remember—but I'm sure it was when he came in with coal. He always took care of that."

Miss Maud's words exploded in a burst of breath. "He was in here the evening before Louise died—I mean the evening before the evening, that's the day before, and even stopped to talk awhile which is not like George at all; he usually just says a word or two and goes on but that evening he stopped to talk and then the next morning he didn't show up at all and I had to get my own coal and then that night was when Louise—that's Mrs. Crayley, died and—poor darling ..."

The sheriff and his deputy had been staring, almost hypnotized it seemed, at Miss Maud. Finally then, it evidently dawned on the sheriff that this might turn out to be permanent, and he widened his hanging mouth and said, "Uhhh ..." loudly, and then, "Excuse me please. What did George talk about? Did he say anything about going away for awhile?"

Miss Maud's eyes glowed. So few questions were ever offered to her. "Let me see now—I don't believe he said a word about going anywhere no, what he wanted to talk about was Tina that's Lance's new wife, he wanted to know if I'd seen Tina before because he had, he said—but he said he couldn't remember where..." The sheriff said, "Uhhh ..." and turned to Ellen. "Mr. Crayley's wife. Is she in the house?"

"Yes, so far as I know," Ellen said. "Would you like to see her?"

"Please."

"... but it was an idle kind of talk and I didn't pay much attention because if you ask me, George just took a notion to leave and I've heard old men get odd notions sometimes and mercy knows George was odd enough before he was ever old and ..."

Ellen closed the door firmly on Miss Maud's continued information.

Tina was coming down the wide front stairs dressed in a black and white pantsuit that complimented her figure and her complexion. She smiled when she saw Ellen, but as always, to Ellen the smile seemed more mocking than friendly.

"The sheriff wants to see you," Ellen said.

Tina stopped, her eyebrows raised, her eyes going smoky dark and wandering away thoughtfully as if counting possibilities. She shrugged and smiled again at Ellen, and went ahead of her down the hall.

"Mrs. Crayley," the sheriff said, "We'd like to know if you've seen or know anything about George Miller."

The smile was still on Tina's face. "George Miller?"

"Yes," the sheriff answered, his voice softened. "He's the elderly man who worked here. He seems to have disappeared."

Ellen glanced at Rodney and saw that his eyes were steady and narrowed, watching Tina. She turned away so she would not see and pretended to be busy at the cabinet where Miss Maud always had an assortment of things to keep busy with.

She heard Tina's high-pitched, child's voice say, "Oh. I remember him. He's the old man who brought in the coal. Should I have seen him, Sheriff? I mean, I think I did see him a couple of times, but that's all. I didn't even know his name."

"Well," the sheriff said, his voice accompanied by a footstep toward the door. "Then I see no reason to keep these ladies."

"I'm sorry I couldn't help you, Sheriff," Tina said. "Well, these things happen. An old man can go for a walk and drop over with a heart attack—or just plain forget where he is and wander off. We'll just go out and look around the place a while longer."

Ellen didn't look up to see them go, but she knew that Rodney was the last of the three men, the one to shut the door. Without saying anything more Tina went back into the hall, the door slamming behind her. Ellen found herself thinking that in many more ways than one, Tina was like a child. Even to the careless way she usually closed a door.

A bit later she decided to get out of the house, go shopping, anything, and went into the back stairs hall to get a coat. The moment she closed the door and stepped into the quiet of the small room at the foot of the stairs she heard the chime, sounding just the way it had in the beginning, faint and far, far away. Just a tiny bell in the distance. She paused, listened, and changed her direction. Instead of the closet door she went to the foot of the stairs and looked up. The chime was moving again, after several days and nights, and something Miss Maud had said occurred to her. Tina might be doing it. She could have stepped into the closet the other day, or behind a heavy chest. Ellen hadn't thought of that at the time. Now she had to know.

She stooped quickly, pushed off her shoes, and then moved soundlessly up the stairs. On the second flight of stairs she slowed. The increasing cold made her shiver, yet it was more than the cold. The bell sound had changed to the thin flute voice calling Tin-a, Tin-a. It swept through her, increasing her chills, and she thought of turning back. Yet she had to see, to make sure about Tina.

All the bedroom doors were closed, but the direction of the voice was unmistakable. She went to the door of the small bedroom and forced herself to open the door, quietly but quickly. She pushed it wide open and stepped across the threshold in one movement. The chime swung wildly on its string, and at close range gave out many more tinkles than she had heard downstairs, sounds soft and lilting. Someone had given it a hard push, yet Tina was not there.

No longer bothering to be quiet Ellen ran to the closet door and jerked it open. Cold, musty air burst upon her, but the closet was empty. She left the door open and turned, looking behind the chests, even under the bed. Then she ran to the next bedroom and the next, to come finally back into the hall, breathless. The chime still tinkled and with it the thin far away voice calling Tin-a, Tin-a.

Tina was not there. No one was there. Ellen went back to the small bedroom and stood staring at the swinging chime. As she watched, the breadth of the swing increased and the chime swung wider and wider, beginning to sound like glass breaking and crashing, and through it all the strange and weird call, *Tin-a*.

Footsteps on the stairs then brought something tangible and welcome. Ellen ran into the hall hoping to see Miss Maud.

Tina stood on the stairs, looking up. There was no smile on her face now. Only an annoyed frown. "What are you doing? How are you doing that?" she demanded.

Suddenly Ellen knew, without understanding, whatever it was that had come to live in the bedroom wanted Tina. "No," she cried, holding to the railing, leaning over and looking down at Tina, "Don't come up here. Whatever you do don't come up here!"

In the slight pause Ellen heard silence. Only the wind whined under the eaves. The chime was still at last. Then Tina's laughter filled the silence.

"Are you nuts? This house is as much mine as yours. Maybe more. I can go into any room I wish!" She began to climb again, determined.

"You don't understand what I mean!" Ellen cried. "Please listen —I didn't call you. It's the chime that did it. It's the chime, Tina!"

Tina had reached the landing and faced Ellen, anger snapping in her eyes. "What chime?"

Ellen pointed toward the bedroom. "In there—but ..." Tina was already going toward the open door and Ellen reached out to stop her. "Don't go in there, please!"

Tina twisted away, went on into the room and stood looking at the wind chime. Slowly her face broke into amusement. She giggled. "I'll be damned. This old chime!" Ellen followed her, but her eyes covered the corner in amazement. The chime hung limp and still as if it had never moved.

Tina went closer, looking up. "That's the silliest story I ever heard, Ellen. But I'll tell you something—you'd better stop playing with this thing or you might break it, and you must never, never break it or something terrible will happen." One finger raised almost to touch a sliver of glass but stopped a bare inch away.

Ellen watched in silence as Tina went to the door, but instead of leaving Tina stopped and looked again at the chime.

"Do you know where it came from?" she asked.

"The chime?" Ellen answered. "It has always been here."

"So it's not yours?"

"No."

"I didn't think so. It's much too cheap and shabby to ever have belonged to you. I expect the person it belonged to must have been very cheap and shabby too, don't you think?"

"I think they might have been my mother's," Ellen said softly.

"Oh really?" Tina's eyes came to rest on her. "Where did she get them?"

"I don't know."

"You don't know anything at all about it, or about your mother, or anything, do you?"

"No."

"Too bad," Tina said, smiling her teasing, taunting smile. "I expect there were some things your granny could have told you, but it's too late now, isn't it?" Laughing, Tina went down the stairs, and

Ellen remained where she was, puzzled at Tina's behavior, listening to the light, quick steps.

Then Tina's voice, raised nearly to shouting, came back to her. "Why don't you ask your father? If I were you, I'd make him tell me where that chime came from. But I'll make a bet with you, Ellen baby —I'll bet he won't tell you a thing!"

## CHAPTER 7

Rodney stood by the ranch office, hands in pockets, ears beginning to freeze in the cold north wind, and watched the sheriff's car leave. So far it seemed to have been a wasted afternoon. The sheriff couldn't think of anything he hadn't already thought of, except one. Amnesia. The old man might have had a lapse of memory and simply wandered off. If that were the case, the law might be able to find him.

Rodney glanced at the house, at the rows of windows on the second floor, and wondered which room was Ellen's. The beautiful little girl with the shining dark braids, the little princess in her castle, who grew up to be—ummm. He used to see her face against the third story window once in awhile. But no more. Either she wasn't interested enough to look for him out her window, or she had moved. George said she'd moved. He hoped that was the deal.

In the office, the closed door rattling in the wind, Rodney threw off his jacket and put the coffee on to heat. Then he sat down at his desk and wondered again why Ellen had stopped coming to the office. She seemed to be avoiding him since her grandmother's funeral.

That grave on the hill was one of the things he hadn't mentioned to the sheriff. Or even that George had told him, too, that he had seen Lance's wife somewhere. He got up and ran his fingers through his hair. Sometimes he felt there was some connection there that was more than George's imagination, something to do with Tina, and with the grave. But so far he hadn't been able to figure it out.

He poured the coffee and sat down again and picked up a yellow pencil to twist it idly in his fingers. He pulled facts out of his mind again, piece by piece, trying to make sense of them. First, Albert had gone to South America on business. But a few days before he left, Ellen came home. He didn't know anyone on the whole ranch who wasn't glad to make the trade. Everything was fine then. He was fine, George was fine. Mrs. Crayley was fine. Fair, at least. George was fine until the day he carried the pictures down for Ellen. Then he began to worry about Ellen's mother. About what had happened to her. And he had gotten that bug about digging up the grave.

Then the day of Mrs. Crayley's funeral Ellen put that festering thought in his own mind. The grave had been disturbed. Or had it? He didn't know. The one time he had started off to look at it again, Tina had followed him into the meadow. He wound up taking her for a walk instead because he sure didn't want any of the family to know what he had in mind. What George had had in mind. About the grave.

And Tina. He thought now that George might have been right about the cathouse, because if ever a woman was on the make, it was Tina. Wife of Lance. Poor devil. Rodney had tried, every time he saw her, to draw her out, find out where she came from. But she was tight as hell on information. She had met Lance in Las Vegas, she told that much. But when he asked, "Las Vegas the old hometown?" she laughed and said, "No, I'm a traveling girl." She kept laughing, and after a moment said, "You wouldn't believe it!" It sounded like a remark the boys used to make, like, *Man, rough riding weather,* that was half joke and half truth. And he got the idea she wouldn't be saying any more about it.

He couldn't figure her out. There was something about her that made him uneasy. Entirely aside from the fact that he didn't want to mess around with her because she was Lance's wife, for one thing, and because she didn't appeal to him, for another. But mostly because he didn't want to lose what little he had of Ellen.

He got his jacket, zipped it up, and headed for the back door of the bunkhouse. Maybe Tina wouldn't see him this time. Though she seemed to have a divining rod on her because, no matter where he was, she usually turned up.

Keeping the buildings, and then the trees, between himself and the house, Rodney went around to the sloping west side of Crayley Hill and climbed, long steps that took him quickly to the top. He had no trouble finding the grave again. And looking at it, squatting on his heels to stay out of sight, he sifted sand through his fingers and wondered if he had been dreaming the other time. Had it just been an optical illusion that the grave had seemed slightly rounded? Or had someone smoothed it and leveled it since then? He didn't bother the tumbleweeds that had piled against the stone. They would only pile up again. He stood up and stepped backwards into the shadows of a cedar, and then went down the hill toward the bunkhouse.

She was waiting for him in the office, burrowed into the richness of the fur coat. She smiled, reminding him of a small, sharp-eyed animal. "Where have you been?" she asked. Though she still smiled, the question seemed querulous.

He smiled too, trying to hide his annoyance at finding her in his office. "I do work, you know." He slung the jacket over the back of his chair, sat down and put both feet on the desk. Sprinkles of sand fell, but he didn't move the feet.

"Do you!" she said, which was a challenge, not a question. Her face was suddenly sober. "Who brought the sheriff?"

"I did."

"Because the old man is missing?"

"That's right."

"I didn't think Albert had." She came over and put her hand on the back of his neck, and cold chills moved down his spine. "Why don't you stop worrying about him? He was old."

"So he may need help. He may be lost somewhere." Though he couldn't imagine George lost. He moved and got to his feet to get away from her hand. Because he had kissed her once didn't mean he'd sold his soul to her. He put one hand in the middle of her furred back and pushed her toward the door. "I do have work to catch up on. I seem to have lost my secretary."

"I'll help you." She was turning, her hands coming up and clasping behind his head.

He stood stiff and unyielding, wondering the best way to handle her and get rid of her without much damage done. He could have kicked himself in the teeth for giving in to that one kiss. "Look, Mrs. Crayley," he said, no smile now, no teasing. "I do have work to do, so if you'll excuse me ..." He firmly disentangled her fingers and removed her hands from his neck. They were small hands, and cold as the winter wind. But her face was hot and furious. He saw the anger building.

She didn't move. She looked steadily into his eyes, her breath growing fast and shallow. Her nostrils flared, and drew in tight and white-edged. So much like a furious wild stallion, he thought in astonishment. Was that how she controlled people? With anger?

"You're not in love with *her*," she said, and there was no question whom she meant. He didn't like her sneering tone.

"Not that it's any of your business," he said, "but yes, I am."

The hatred and the fury was all over her, and he saw that it was she who was being controlled. She jerked the fur coat around her and started out, throwing the door back against the wall with all her strength. He thought she was leaving, and he was glad of that, but she had one more thing to say.

"Good!" Her voice shook, just under a scream. The wind tore her white hair loose and swept strands of it forward around her face, and for a horrible moment she looked just like a picture of a witch he had seen once. "I'm glad you are! Do you hear that, Mr. Ranch Manager? I'm glad you are! And I hope you suffer like hell!"

He stood in the open door and watched her run toward the house. The only thing to do with a woman like that, he thought, was stay out of her way. Forget her. Dismiss her from his mind. Drink his coffee before it froze in the cup. Shut the damned door. In disgust he took his cup, and the coffee pot, and dumped all the old, cold black coffee down the sink.

By evening the strong north wind was bringing hard-driven spots of snow that felt like fine nails hammered into the skin. The weatherman on the six o'clock news was crying a warning to cattlemen. By six-thirty Rodney had Smith and Penroy on their way in the jeep to the north cattle station. The dog went along, shivering but happy to go. The last man, O'Neil, settled down by the fire and the television set.

For awhile Rodney wandered the path between the office door, where he had a porch light burning into the blowing snow, and the stove where O'Neil sat. Every time he looked into what could become the first really bad storm of the winter he saw George out there somewhere, unprotected, and he knew he couldn't wait for the sheriff. Going over the bare facts again he came up with the same puzzle—the picture of Ellen's mother. George's obsession with the grave. And the fact that Tina's face disturbed him.

Had George lost his mind all of a sudden and then wandered off and lost himself entirely, or had he run onto something that no one was supposed to know?

Rodney grabbed his coat, told O'Neil goodnight, and went out into the snow-studded dark. The house was about two hundred yards ahead. A few long, narrow windows were lighted and looked like yellow slits in a black blanket.

Miss Maud was in the kitchen putting dishes away. The first Rodney saw of her was a pair of round eyes bugging at the door he opened.

"Hello, Miss Maud, how are you this evening?"

"Good Lord Rodney, I thought you must be a ghost of George coming in that door, I didn't hear a step or anything, the wind is so strong there's bound to be a blizzard yet you just watch it will be as bad as that one I forgot what year it was but it ..."

Rodney tuned her partly out and sipped the coffee she poured for him. He let her talk for awhile, then he began his systematic interruptions.

"Is Ellen home?"

"... the snow was four feet deep on the—what? Yes, Ellen is home you surely don't think she's so stupid she'd go out on a date on a night like this, poor Louise poor dear, her grave will be covered I suppose or swept bare since it's on the north side of the stone but you just watch now and mind what I say there's going to be an old-fashioned blizzard; if I had my things packed I'd go south for the rest of the winter now that Louise is gone poor ..."

"Just exactly what did George say to you about Lance's wife?"

"... sunshine all winter and he didn't say much just what I told the sheriff, George came in here and asked me if I'd ever seen Tina before and I didn't know what he was talking about then he said he had, like it was something bad or something but he couldn't remember anyway, he's gone now so maybe he remembered all of a sudden and decided to leave before *she* recognized *him.*"

Rodney smiled on one side of his mouth. Yes, that would be like George, especially if it had been the cat-house where he had met her. He had been that guilt-stricken. But there was another thing. Rodney asked, "Did you know Ellen's mother?"

"Seems a lot of people are wanting to know if I knew Ellen's mother and the answer is no just like always ..."

"Who else wanted to know?"

"... I didn't know her because she died a year or more before I came, well it was Ellen who wanted to know ..."

"Why did she want to know?" He thought he knew the answer to that one, but he wanted Maud's version.

"... uh—I think it had something to do with that bedroom upstairs you know, that chopped-up bedroom because she was asking about it too ..."

"Where is that bedroom?"

"... the same time well, it's the little bedroom on the third floor the one around the railing to the left when you come to the top of the stairs, the one straight to the right is Ellen's old room then there's another big one but it's the little one she asked about and the way she talked she had never been in it before and she wondered if it had belonged to her mother ..."

"Had it?"

"... but I didn't know and I still don't ..."

"Thanks for the coffee, Miss Maud."

He was out of the kitchen before she could get started again; the pantry and hall doors closed behind him. The hall stretched ahead, softly lit, carpeted, still. The sound of the wind was almost closed out and so was the sound of Miss Maud's voice.

He didn't know where Ellen was. A mumble of sound came from the small sitting room, but it might have been the television. He didn't want to see Tina, or Lance, or even Albert. He thought he would like to see the bedroom Miss Maud had mentioned, and had no doubts he could reach it without being seen, though he had never been farther upstairs than Mrs. Crayley's room. He had gone there several times when she was sick a couple of winters back, but he couldn't remember seeing the stairs to the third story.

His steps were quiet on the hall rugs, which surprised him considering the size of his boots. In the more narrow hall to Albert's office he saw a faint light, and surmised that Albert was there. Near the end of the main hall a wide stairway rose going straight to a landing at the front of the house where tall, narrow, uncurtained windows showed spots of white snow sticking to the glass of storm windows that were never removed. On the landing the stairs branched. He turned to the right and counted ten more steps up to a large hall that was nearly dark. On the other side of the central linen closet the hall from the other side of the stairs joined and they became one, narrowed, going back like a dark tunnel to a dim light that hung above another stairway that went down, dropping out of sight into darkness. A black hole in the wall showed, as he moved closer, a flight of stairs going up.

This stairway was enclosed. Steep, narrow. His hand feeling the wall touched an old push button switch, and another dim light came on far above, in a ceiling so high it looked domed.

Thinking to himself that it was probably a waste of time since he didn't know what he was looking for anyway, he climbed the stairs and stood undecided. Ellen's old room, or the one she had asked about? Ellen's old room first.

It was big, about thirty feet or more square, filled with furniture that must have been built on the spot because he couldn't see how it got up there otherwise. A high, dark ceiling, and dreary dark walls. What a place for a little girl. Or a big one for that matter. And what a contrast with the bedroom in the house he wanted to buy for her, ranch brick on ten acres near town. He wanted to take her to see it, but first he had to ask her that question. And that was where he turned coward.

But anyway, what a hell of a place for a girl like Ellen to live. No wonder she had moved downstairs.

His hand was on the switch, ready to turn out the light, when he glimpsed it. Just a brief glint of reflecting light near one of the big pillows on the bed. He raised the pillow and uncovered what he had doubted he saw—a long, sharp bread knife with blade that tapered to a point, honed and polished with long use. He frowned at it a moment, thinking what a crazy damned place to keep a knife like that.

Was that Ellen's idea of self-protection? From what? Crazy kid. Well at least she left it behind when she moved. He replaced the pillow and left the room as he had found it, with only the tip of the knife blade in sight.

The small room was a bit of a shocker. It didn't take him long to understand why Ellen had started asking about her mother, for the room looked as if it had housed a lunatic.

Thoughtfully he went back down the stairs and turned out the light. He wanted to see Ellen. But what could she tell him? Albert was the one he should ask, for Albert was the only person left who knew the truth about the girl in the picture, the one George had sworn was not Irene Crayley. Albert was the only one left who knew what had happened in the small bedroom. What connection it had with Ellen's mother.

But, as George had said, he couldn't bother the family. Yet George was now missing because he had wanted to open the grave.

Something wriggled and twisted in the back of his thoughts like a worm on a hook, but he couldn't get hold of it. He went down the back stairs, out through the screened porch and back to the bunkhouse.

In his office he sat in the dark and watched lights go on in second story windows, out in the windows downstairs, and finally, total darkness. The snow and wind sounded like weird things screaming around corners and through cracks in the bunkhouse. Finally, Rodney stretched out in his bed and slept.

He woke in a pale, snow-sifted daylight. The wind was still screaming, throwing small-flaked snow against the windows like billions of tiny darts. But it wasn't a real Crayley County blizzard yet. The big house was still faintly visible. And so was Albert's white

Cadillac moving out of the driveway. It would take a whale of a blizzard to keep Albert home from work. He counted two heads in the car and assumed one belonged to Lance. A glance at the clock showed him it was past eight. He felt as if he had slept all day.

O'Neil was gone. Getting coal for the house probably, or doing some early morning cattle feeding. He had left a pot of coffee on the pot belly and a package of sweet rolls on the table. Rodney didn't bother with the rolls. He was testing the coffee when it hit him.

George must have dug into the grave. What he found held the answer to his disappearance.

Rodney zipped his jacket and grabbed a pair of gloves. Ten minutes later he was climbing Crayley's Hill with a pick and a shovel in his hands. He didn't have to worry about being seen because the wind swept the snow straight south toward the house, obscuring its lines so that only the black chimneys were visible.

The ground of the grave was frozen almost brick hard. But, he hoped, it was a shallow freeze. With his back to the wind he began chipping away the hard soil that lay a few inches down. His chest hurt. His throat felt raw. The snow and the wind kept coming with never a let-up. He worked down near the stone, a hole just wide enough to work in. But if a coffin were there at all, he'd find it.

He wasn't prepared for the heavy work shoe his shovel scraped against. For a long, breathless time he stared at the shoe. Not once had he allowed himself to think of that. Finally he bent and with his hands worked the soil away until he could identify the sock above the reddish leather of the shoe. Sick to his stomach, he climbed out of the hole and staggered away, leaving the pick and shovel beside the grave.

At the end of the bunkhouse he stopped and leaned. George dead? George in the grave. Covered. Someone ...

He heard the sound of a motor and looked up. In ghostly outline near the house stood the blue ranch pickup, and going toward it was a tall woman. The pickup roared, spun its wheels and moved slowly away. Rodney stared until it was gone in a burst of wind-driven snow.

He couldn't believe it. Miss Maud going out on a day like this? O'Neil taking her shopping or something? They both must be crazy as hell. He hoped Ellen had had sense enough to stay home.

Rodney blinked against the snow. Miss Maud had predicted a blizzard, and it was coming now. In another few minutes he wouldn't be able to see the road.

He began running toward the long garage where he kept his car. The family couldn't be kept out of it any longer because George had been murdered. But he wanted to tell Albert first. Like George, he couldn't believe Albert was guilty of murder—and yet someone was.

Driving the seven miles to the bank in Crayley required great skill. At times he thought he wouldn't make it; but finally he slid to a stop against the curb in front of the bank. It was usually a no-parking zone, but today there was no one on the snow-flooded streets to object.

He didn't pause to be announced but walked past the surprised secretary and pushed open the door to Albert's office. He was exactly as Rodney expected him to be, erect and occupied with pen and paper at a desk so neat it looked unnatural. And he was gazing up at Rodney with an expression that matched the secretary's.

Rodney leaned down and placed both hands on the desk. "I found George this morning."

Albert Crayley's hazel eyes didn't so much as blink. They widened a trifle. He didn't say a word.

"He's in the grave," Rodney said, his voice rough.

"Grave?"

"Her grave. Ellen's mother's grave."

Albert's face changed color then, and for a moment he looked like a dead man. When he spoke his voice cracked. "How—how did he get there? I don't understand."

"He's been murdered. There's no other way he could have gotten there, because he's covered. There's nothing else in that grave but him, and he's there because he saw that picture that's supposed to be

Irene Crayley and he knew it wasn't. He wouldn't rest until he dug into that grave. Somebody killed him because of it, and who was there to know but you, Mr. Crayley?"

Slowly Albert rose to his feet. He stood as tall as Rodney and Rodney straightened to look into his eyes. But what he saw in Albert Crayley's face was only a groping for understanding.

Rodney said, "I know you didn't kill him, Albert, so who the hell did? I have to go to the sheriff, but I wanted to come here first."

"I—I don't know. There's no one else who knows, now that Mother is gone. No one."

"She couldn't have done it."

"No. No, no. Are you sure about George? How did you find him?"

"I decided to dig into the grave because there was evidence it had been disturbed. His foot ..."

"My God. I just don't understand. There was nothing there and never had been. It was—well, a family thing, a—a very foolish thing probably. Instead of divorcing her I merely did it this way. So there was nothing there. No reason for George to be harmed. None. My God, I don't understand."

To see Albert breaking before his eyes forced Rodney to seek a new calm and strength.

"He didn't want to hurt the family," Rodney said. "Because you'd been good to him. He only wanted to know about the grave for his own peace of mind. After he saw the picture."

"I can understand that," Albert said. "I forgot that George had seen Irene several times. The picture was Mother's idea, because Ellen wanted to know about her all the time when she was small. She adored her mother. I never thought George would see it. There has to be another reason why he was killed. Could he have fallen in? Could it have been an accident?"

"He was covered," Rodney said.

"Oh yes, yes. *Why?* There must have been another reason."

Rodney shook his head, and then he remembered. "The only other thing that bothered him, if you don't mind my saying so, was Lance's wife."

"Lance's wife?"

"Yes. He thought he had seen her somewhere. He was positive he had. But he couldn't remember."

"Tina?"

Again Rodney watched the change in Albert's face. The white blankness. He looked cold as death itself. The word came out in a harsh whisper. *"Tina."* He stared at Rodney, but only half aware. "It can't be. *My God, Mary Lou.* "

"What?" Rodney said. "Who?"

Albert's hand moved and then hung still at his sides. "Where is she now? Where's Ellen?"

Rodney saw the urgency in Albert's face, but he didn't know what he was talking about. "She's at home, I hope."

"Tina!" Albert cried. "Where is Tina?"

"She's ..." Rodney paused briefly, his thoughts flashing to the upstairs bedroom and the knife under the pillow. "She's there too."

"And Maud? For God's sake, man, tell me who is with Ellen?"

Rodney turned without answering and ran. When he reached his car he found that Albert was behind him, his overcoat forgotten. He turned the switch and pressed hard on the accelerator. The engine was roaring before he slammed the door. Albert, beside him, leaning forward, staring into the blinding blizzard, kept saying, "Hurry, for God's sake hurry!" The tires spun, the car slid sideways against the curb and hung there, tires whirling uselessly.

All Rodney could think of was Ellen, the knife, and seven miles of blizzard-bound road back to the ranch.

# CHAPTER 8

Ellen ran down the back stairs and through the small, chopped-up rooms that served as halls and closets. Miss Maud would know why Rodney had driven off in a storm that was increasing almost to blizzard conditions. His car had spun wildly sideways at the turn onto the main road, in a way that increased her feeling of uneasiness. She watched him from her window as far as she could see, and then went in search of Miss Maud. She seemed to know almost everything that went on. She would probably know the reason for Rodney's reckless hurry.

"Miss Maud ..." She stopped, the swinging door behind her rocking into stillness. The storm was louder here, beating at the windows, emphasizing the silence. Not even a light burned to alleviate the gray emptiness of the kitchen.

At the far end a door stood open. Ellen went to it and looked into the room that was Miss Maud's private sitting room. No light burned there, either.

"Miss Maud," she called again, louder. There still was no answer. Ellen walked slowly into the small sitting room, and from that into the bedroom. A piece of paper pinned to the pillow drew her attention. Miss Maud's handwriting was as horse-like as her long-legged stride. Ellen read it softly aloud.

"Dear Ellen. Sorry I had to leave before you returned but like Tina said if I'm going south this winter it looks like I'd better hurry and go. O'Neil will drive me to town. See you in the spring. Love, Maud."

Ellen looked about the room in astonishment. "Returned! But I haven't been anywhere." She spread her palms in a confused gesture and tried to laugh. Returned? Miss Maud wrote as if she had been gone, yet they had seen each other only a few hours earlier, at breakfast. And now Miss Maud was gone for the winter. Without a goodbye—only a strange little note.

The room seemed then to be uncomfortably still, almost haunted, and Ellen went back into the kitchen. She found it no better. All around her, closed into the dark old house, was an odd kind of silence, the absence of Miss Maud's comfortable and constant ramblings almost deafening. The storm was all that was left.

Ellen stood in the center of the forty feet of kitchen length and listened to the faint groans and creaks of the house. Her father and Uncle Lance had gone early to work, much against Lance's wishes. But after a talk with Tina he had gone on. Rodney had gone, and now Miss Maud was gone. If it were not for Tina she would be entirely alone. For the first time she felt really glad that Tina was in the house.

She went to the window and looked out. Visibility was so bad now that the men probably would not be able to get back. The outside world was grey-white and featureless. Not even the nearby coal shed could be seen.

The kitchen had grown unpleasant and cold, the fire in the stove so far gone that it was scarcely warm to the touch. She went through the pantry into the hall, and then to the sitting room, followed by the emptiness of her own steps. Tina was not there and Ellen wondered if she too had gone, if the house were to be her only companion in the storm. The house and whatever had come to live in the third story.

As if in answer to her thoughts, Tina's voice came faintly from somewhere above, calling, "Ellen. Come here, Ellen."

Instead of shouting a reply Ellen ran up the front stairs to the second floor.

Tina called again, "Ellen. Ellen," in a singing tone that brought a rush of shivers up Ellen's arms, it seemed so strangely similar to that unreal bell that called for Tina.

"Yes," she answered, preferring her own shout to Tina's continued calls.

But when she knocked on the bedroom door no one answered. Again came the call from above.

"Ellen. Ellen."

Ellen's eyes went toward the third story stairway, so nearly dark in the thickening storm, and chills spread over her body.

"I'm coming," she answered. But at the foot of the stairs she paused to call, "What is it, Tina?"

"Come up here, Ellen.

Ellen started up, then hesitated. She had asked Tina not to go up, but she had gone anyway. Maybe there was really nothing there, after all. Yet ... "No. Please come down Tina, please. Let's go downstairs."

"In a minute. Come on up. I have something for you."

"What is it?"

"It's a surprise, Ellen. I can't tell you."

"Will you come down then?"

"Yes. Then I'll come down."

Ellen took another step and paused. There was something about the voice that was different. It was Tina's voice—and yet it seemed more child-like than ever, more conjuring. For a moment she considered that it might not be Tina at all. It might be the other thing, the bell, calling for her now. She stepped backwards one step, away from whatever awaited her in the third story.

But then came impatient footsteps on the floor above and Tina yelling in a normal voice, "Ellen! Are you coming up or aren't you?"

"All right," Ellen replied, climbing, "I'll be right there."

Tina's footsteps went back into the bedroom, Ellen's old room, and when Ellen reached the landing she unhesitatingly followed.

She was surprised then to find Tina was not in the room.

Ellen stood between the door and the bed, and asked in a voice soft and wary, "Tina? Are you here?"

The storm beat against the walls, the window, the roof, its shrill voice the only sound in the world. Slowly, Ellen approached the bed, her gaze going to the chest near the corner where the small body of a nine or ten year old child could hide. Though it was mid-day the room was as dark as the room in her nightmares. Just as slowly then, Ellen began backing toward the door. Something was wrong. She wouldn't speak again or make a sound of any kind. The desire to run was building in her, yet she didn't dare make a sound.

A figure sprang suddenly from behind the door, black hair streaming loose down each side of the white diamond face, one hand raised like a claw, the other holding something long and bright. The cry that came from the twisted mouth rang through the high ceilinged rooms, echoing Ellen's cry of surprise.

In the silence that followed Ellen stood nearly paralyzed staring at the dark-haired girl. "*Mary Lou*," she whispered in horror, feeling her lips move and no more sound escaping. She was seeing the girl of her nightmares come to life before her, and through her fear came the exploding memory. Many memories. There had been a young girl in the house, a real girl, and the hatred had been as real as the threat that poured from the girl's lips now.

"I've come back to kill you, Ellen."

The question *why?* came to Ellen and the realization that there was no sane answer to it. Now, as then, the answer lay somewhere in the depths of the girl's mind, and perhaps not even there. That made the threat all the more deadly. Ellen knew she would have to fight for her life. She was not prepared.

Eyes like burnt holes came toward her, the black hair swung forward, the body arched, and the hand with the knife slowly raised.

Ellen turned and ran for the stairway. She felt the sting of the blade in her left shoulder as Tina pushed between her and the stairs to cut her off from escape. There was nowhere to go then but the door that was nearest, the door to the room where the girl had once lived. The girl followed quickly, driven by the need to kill, and suddenly Ellen was trapped in the small room with her.

Ellen swung around to fight for the knife, to throw it away, and her hand closed over the blade. It sliced through her palm as Tina wrenched it away, and Ellen stumbled backwards into the corner, falling to the floor.

The wind chime was beginning to swing above her, as if driven by a powerful gale that seemed to have broken through from the storm outside, and the voice from the chime came in from far away to throb deafeningly in the room. Tin-a —Tin-a—*Tin-a*.

"No!" Tina screamed, putting her hands to her ears, the knife clutched tightly in her fist. "No! Stop it!"

In a burst of fury her arm swung high and the blade of the knife sliced through the string that held the chime. The glass crashed against the wall, shattering to the floor, and the scream from Tina as she ran into the hall was of unearthly terror.

Ellen stared at the chime, for it seemed in her intense fear that it floated softly and slowly down, the glass tinkles whispering away into the storm like the soft murmurs of many little voices.

The sound of a body falling down the stairs was all that was left then, and the sound of the storm.

Ellen was alone. The wind chime lay broken at her side. Warm blood ran into the sleeve of her sweater. Her hand throbbed with each beat of her heart.

She got to her feet and went with careful, cautious steps into the hall and halfway down the stairs. The body was on the floor at the foot of the stairway, and from beneath it the blood flowed.

Somewhere below a door slammed, and the voices of her father and Rodney called her name. But she couldn't answer. She leaned trembling against the wall and stared at the body on the floor. Something soft and caressing as a gentle touch moved along her cheek and then was gone.

When Rodney reached her she was weeping soundlessly. He picked her up in his arms and carried her, while she pressed her face into the protective warmth of his open jacket, and held to him with all the strength in her arms.

She heard her father's voice. "Well, she's dead. She fell on the knife, I guess." He sounded relieved, but a deep sadness moved in Ellen.

Rodney kept going, carrying her on and down the last flight of stairs.

"There's this little house I found that I want to show you, Ellen," he was saying.

# OTHER NOVELS BY RUBY JEAN

1974 *The House that Samael Built*
1974 *Seventh All Hallows' Eve*
1974 *House at River's Bend*
1975 *The Girl Who Didn't Die*
1978 *Child of Satan's House*
1978 *Satan's Sister*
1978 *Dark Angel*
1982 *Hear the Children Cry*
1982 *Such a Good Baby*
1983 *The Lake*
1983 *MaMa*
1985 *Home Sweet Home*
1985 *Best Friends*
1986 *Wait and See*
1987 *Annabelle*
1987 *Chain Letter*
1988 *Smoke*
1988 *House of Illusions*

1988 *Jump Rope*
1989 *Pendulum*
1989 *Death Stone*
1990 *Vampire Child*
1990 *Lost and Found*
1990 *Victoria*
1991 *Celia*
1991 *Baby Dolly*
1992 *The Reckoning*
1993 *The Living Evil*
1994 *The Haunting*
1995 *Night Thunder*
2022 *Bear Hollow Charlie*
2022 *Cry of the Soul*
2022 *Pride of Bella Terra*